AF373473

# The Hustler`s Story Never Die

## By Thapelo Edwin Potsanyane;

## Email: thapelopotsanyane@gmail.com

## Tel: +266 50924517

## About the book

This book is about a man called TP who is willing to give up everything to attain freedom of the people of his country. He is the master mind behind the toppling of the dictatorship government that governed Lesotho at the time. Things began going the opposite side from what he anticipated, as people closer to him began being murdered and those people he thought he could trust began betraying him. But he is willing to fight back, together with his two friends Emm and Justice, went through a hard time but we're willing to fight and protect the new government which took place after the dictators were toppled.

They believed in new government and worked hard to eliminate Judas who was now working with the opposition party to assassinate the new prime minister. But it seemed they were just getting started after eliminating him as his funders or bosses began looting the resources of the country, so TP and friends had to hunt them too, their other friend Emm die along the way as things get worse, but they can't stop fighting for their country.

**N: B** the book in all the chapters' starts with the end and end with the way it should have started. Part one where TP is a professor is just an imagination and fantasy of him as he tells his friends in the cave, this is illustrated well in part two of the book where he tells his two friends Emm and Justice that the professor story is just a dream he hopes to achieve one day.

## Marketing plan

I am a new author, I don't know much about marketing a book, but I wish to market it in all social media platforms like Facebook etc. And displayed in all the readers networks in the form of soft copies or it can even be converted to an audio book.

## Future plans

I wrote one book and self published it in Amazon's but I couldn't promote it because of lack of money. My future plans are to write more fictional books, and at least have four books in two years to come.

# PART 1

**Summary of part 1 and chapter 1 to 6**

This part entails chapters whereby TP who is the main character is a professor of social work profession and in his carrier he has office where by he deals with clients on daily basis. But most of the time clients that come to his office are adults, so on Monday the 19th he was visited by three young adults at their twenties. And their names are Mrs Rethabile Lepeo, Mrs Lineo Maope and Mr. Thabo Rantsi, who are all third year social work students at the National University. So Professor is glad to come across such young people, they want to know about the life story of Prof and what he did to achieve the position he is on at the time. This part one of the conversations between professor and his visitors takes four days from Monday to Thursday.

**Summary of chapter one**

Prof TP welcomes three youth, two ladies (Rethabile, nicknamed Retha and Lineo) and a gentleman (Thabo), they want to know more about him, so he starts first by telling them where he was born and his life when growing up. Being raised by his single mother 'Mathapelo who lived with them and worked hard to make sure they do no sleep with an empty stomach. He describes how his mother is his hero as she played a major role in his life. We see where their conversation get interrupted by Maria who is the secretary of Prof telling him about many clients who are waiting for him outside but he cancels his appointments for the whole week so that he could be with this young souls. The chapter ends where he tells them they should stop for the day, as he wants them to go read.

# Chapter 1

Everything was clear, the sky was blue, and the sun shined brightly up in the sky, birds of the air flew magically catching their prey above. Outside his office, so much noise from people outside and from car engines could be heard. Just outside his office is the main road, clustered with vehicles and people moving up and down, creating such a disturbing noise it was hard to concentrate, hence he immediately stopped writing.

His office was so tidy, every day he would take a cloth from his briefcase after venturing in, dust his shoes, and fasten his tie properly. Before putting his briefcase down on the table he would dust it, arrange everything in order; pens into pen box etc. reboot his computer to check mails from partnering companies. That was each morning`s routine, everyday his office was overflowing with clients from far away communities and districts of the country. They all came for one thing; to seek knowledge and skills on how to battle the problems that came with life itself.

It was a Monday morning, the 19th of august when some ladies and a gentleman came visiting professor TP's office. Since it was such a beautiful Monday, he hanged his beloved suit around his chair and loosened a tie around his neg. the room was silent, only a click, click sound from his computer could be heard. The office door was lightly opened, as this young souls knocked at the door, with a smile; prof- `come in`...

And he offered them chairs. He was glad to come across young clients, most people who visited his office were people aged thirty-seven and upwards, so it was very surprising to come across those clients who were at their early twenties, hence that put a huge smile on his face and the young souls felt very much welcome. They introduced themselves starting with ladies as the young man said; "ladies firs t", they smiled and the first one, who was brown skinned, short hair, brown eyes, a very good looking young lady introduced herself as Rethabile Lepeo, she was from Semonkong in the Maseru district, she was on her third year at the National University of Lesotho doing her BA Social Work.

The second one was short, had a very nice voice, long Brazilian hair, with a light skin tone; they call them yellow bones! She was a third year student too; her name is Lineo Maope from ty in the Berea district. The last guy was the one who said "ladies first", he seemed very naughty, he didn't have much to say, he introduced himself proudly as Mr Thabo Rantsi from Mokhotlong, he was also a third year student at NUL. They were all from NUL doing their third year in Social work profession.

Prof- "You are welcome guys; feel at home` he then proceeded-`how may I be of service to you today? Thabiso, 'Eh! Actually prof we are here to ask about your live, how you grew up and how did you come to this successful ladder? one day we wish to be where you are'.

Professor's mind rewind back to the days as young as seven years old, when life was beautiful, everything was green, to the young winter and summer were alike, poverty and richness had no difference, life was easy because everything was done by parents. In his spiritual eye he could see himself, his younger brother Katleho, going to school, back and forth and everything was just tranquil.

He then cut the thinking and looked into the young faces in front of him.

`Thank you my children for visiting me today, I rarely have visitors as young as yourselves, I am really humbled`. The room was peaceful, everyone listened attentively, small note pats in their hands, and ball pens were held tidily ready to write. Their focus and attention was on professor. In their eyes he could for-see youths with dreams, hunger for success was written in their faces. Their will to hustle humbled his soul and he went on by clearing his throat, the tone of his voice was beginning to deplete due to old age so he had to gather some strength as it might take him time to talk to the young ones.

As he was about to talk, his secretary Maria knocked at the door and he invited her in; She told prof that more clients were waiting for him outside. He asked her; "Maria could you please cancel all my appointments for this week. I really have very important people to deal with these days". Maria obeyed and closed the door behind her. They (girls and a boy) were flattered at the way they were being treated.

Prof- 'where were we'?

Thabiso jumped first- 'you were about to begin sir', with a big smile on his face he said that, looking straight into professor's eyes.

Prof- 'Alright then, let us start from the beginning; everything needs a foundation to develop into a better structure that the builder wants. But before that, can you guys tell me what you do before planting a tree'?

Rethabile raised a hand and said- "one should dig a hole first and put a tree inside".

Prof- 'you are right Retha! For a tree to grow well and be what the grower wants it to be, it should have a foundation, so that its roots can fit in and with this you see; the roots of a young tree would penetrate the earth to pull water and nutrients for it to grow well. Even the grower himself would intern water and feed a tree some manure for it to grow properly.

Same thing applies with the builders of houses or other big structures like bridges, whether small or big, they first have to dig a foundation and then they start implanting or building whatever they want in that foundation`. At the moment, the room was silent, only the voice and echoes of professor could be heard; the young ones listened attentively without writing a thing. It could be seen from their eyes they were amazed at the parables professor was telling them. He could see in their eyes that they were listening but confused on how trees and buildings were connected to the question they asked him.

To clear the confusion, he proceeded.

-`for all starts with the foundation and it seem therefore that, nothing without the foundation can last, so is the life we live in. Everyone has their own foundation and this come in the form of the background, where we come from and the way we were raised when we were young`. Their faces cleared; it seemed they were now getting prof`s point.

Prof-`I was born in this mountainous kingdom, in the rural areas of Maseru in Semonkong, this is the birth place of my mother 'Mathapelo, I was born in one Methodist hospital in Semonkong. It is no more a hospital but a home for the Orphans and the vulnerable. In the year nineteen ninety three (1993), my mother delivered me into this cruel world`.

-`I always agree with many people who say; this world is not for the weak but for the hustlers, I was born a hustler for I was born in the family of hustlers. My home place (being my father`s home) is Ngope-ts`oeu in the same district, about forty kilometres (40km) from Maseru town. After I was born, my mom took me home. I was told that during those days, my mother`s mom being my grandma passed on, my grandfather being my brother`s brother also died; then I was named; Lefu (death) by my mom`s family and Thapelo (Prayer), nicknamed TP, by my father`s family.

Life has never been easy! For no one promised it would be easy`.

-`Growing up I always wondered how come other children live with all their parents and live happily while I only lived with my mom. But there was not an explanation because I was still young; my mind was not going to be able to cope with the burden of the explanations they might give me. So I waited until my mind came to a point of appreciating between the right and wrong. To assess and analyse what was really going on around me. That's life! We were only three in the family i.e. my mom, my younger bro and I, you see, there was no father. As I grew up I realized my mom was the only hustler in our lives`.

-`She used to wake up early in the morning each day; at the time we had moved to Maseru nearer to the town to the place called Hamatala; sure you know the place! Day in and day out mother would wake up early in the morning and go into the street to sell some bananas and apples and other things to make some ends meet. It was a very tough life but like I said earlier; no one promised anyone that it would be easy. All we have to do is just hustle forward.

-No one choose to be born in the families they are into, life chooses it for us, but what it does not choose is our destiny. Since it chooses our foundations, it is there for up to us and our caregivers as children or young people to build good into those foundations so as to be the persons we would wish to be`.

When you are a child, understanding the lives our parents go through isn't that easy, we just appreciate when we look like other kids, brag that we have new shoes or clothes, without even knowing how come we have those. Each morning and each night our parents cry endlessly when they look at us. Pain of deep love for their kids, for them to have a better future, we see them cry each day but because at that stage we do not understand the power of their love to us, it just by pass our minds.

-`My mom was one of those rare women who would do whatever it takes to make sure we do not go to bed with an empty stomach, some days she would brew some traditional bear for local folks to come and buy and hence she was able to pay a monthly rent, she was able to buy us school books and uniform and we wouldn't go to school shearing tears of hunger`.

-She is my hero-

`Everyone has a hero in life, a role model, that person you wish to follow on their foot-steps, not that I wanted to be poor because my mom was poor, but because she was a hustler, she would do anything to get what she wanted, the pure heart she had, a clear mind she possessed drove me to say "I want to be like her, have a good heart, a loving, caring, and a helping mentality, I would do anything for my kids to achieve their goals,  I would do anything for those who are willing to hustle to achieve that which they are hustling for".

-"gentleman, ladies; are you with me?" Professor tapped a little on the table… everyone was so much concentrating and each ones thinking put them in the position to think deep about their lives, their parents and caregivers, their lives as they grew up, their thinking got astray. Away in the mountain kingdom, deep in the mountains where they came from, where people live peacefully with the spirit of Ubuntu, where no one would go to sleep with an empty stomach when the neighbours are still around. That's the life the Basotho nation used to have, industrialisation made many lose their culture and norms and many do not know now who they really are.

Professor`s voice was one of the voices everyone would skip their lunch just to listen to what he had to say. When he speaks, you automatically stop whatever you were doing and listen to him. As he was talking, everyone could draw a picture of what he was talking about. They did not even realise that it was after lunch, because they wanted him to say more and more.

Prof- "Guys, are you listening?"

They all stopped what they were busy digesting and said;

-"yes prof we are listening"!

Prof- "I think we should stop here for today, see me tomorrow when you have time".

He could see they were disappointed, they wanted him to go further with the story, but he wanted to give them time to digest what he was saying to them, he also wanted them to have time to study. They then exchanged their goodbyes and vamoosed. It was already late, prof told Maria to go home (sure you remember the secretary) she was one of the beautiful and intelligent young souls professor has ever worked with. She was humble and she would listen attentively when prof talk to her, as a result, she became the apple of prof's eye. He took her as his own daughter and the following year he would be paying her varsity fees to proceed with her studies in social sciences.

Prof and Maria were ready to go, he put on his suit and took the briefcase, switched off the office computer and headed outside. It could be spotted from his face that, his day was epic.

## Summary of Chapter 2

This chapter we see Prof TP at his home early in the morning before he goes to work, and it also introduced his wife 'Makatleho who is a nurse in one private hospital, they have three kids and is a very good family. Prof takes his kid to school as other two children were at the University, at home only one left so he drops him to school as he pass to work. Maria (the secretary) Thabo, Retha and Lineo were already at the office and they are glad to see professor. He proceeds with the story of his life, he motivates them and tells them about his relationship with his mother and he tells them the stories his mother used to tell him. He tells them that his mother's health was getting worse due to sicknesses but he stops his conversation with them as he remembers he has a meeting with his friends Emm and Justice at Lesotho sun. It has been a long time since they seen each other so this is their very important meeting, the meeting goes well and they part ways as it was too late, promise to come to that spot after every third month. Characters are Prof TP, Thabo and friends, Maria (the secretary), Emm and Justice.

## Chapter 2

After the blackest nights, the sun always rises!

Yes the sun rose the following day, winter breeze swept passed scotched trees, leaves that could be counted fell down one by one from those trees as Prof stood by the window of his double storey house having some coffee, his bedroom window faced directly where the sun came from as it sets its nose onto the earth. Few clouds could be spotted from a distance; he could tell the weather wasn't going to be good that day. It would disappoint him so much because he was looking forward to meeting his new young friends.

His wife, Matlotliso was still asleep; she was a nurse in one private hospital in town in that district of Maseru. They have three kids, the elder one was doing his final year in IT at the University of free state, the second born was a first year at the National University of Lesotho and the last born was tailing his sister in form D. Prof had a very good and supportive family, each weekend the family would gather together at home or go out to have some lunch, he was really a wonderful man.

After finishing his coffee he was ready to leave the house, his wife wasn't feeling well so she would be staying at home that day. The kid was ready for his dad to drop him at school while going to work, the last born; he was very close to his father as he was the only one at home since his brother and sister were at varsity. Soon as they left the house, the weather changed to bad. He concluded in his mind that his friends won`t make it. He drove his boy to school and dropped him, collided fists and he parted to his office, he was very early as he arrived just before eight (8am).

He could tell that Maria was already in the building, so he knocked and he was invited in, he was surprised to realise that Thabo and friends were already there and having a wonderful conversation with Maria. He could tell by the smiles on their faces that they were having a wonderful talk as they enjoyed some cups of coffee. Before he could even greet them, they all greeted him;

-`Morning professor TP

He was flattered; he smiled and returned the greeting;

-`Morning guys, Maria…

He then invited them to the office; they started with small talks of yesterday

Prof- `So guys let us proceed from where we left yesterday…`

-A Smooth sea never made a skilled mariner`- *English proverb*

-`Life is a combination of happiness and sadness, good and bad, problems and achievements, obstacles and goals. All you have to learn in life is to dance in midst of the storm, you see, eagles prefer to fly in storm, why? Because that`s where skill and knowledge lies, where they learn how to dance, hence they fly high above the sky, above the storms they conquer the spaces, this is why they are seen by other birds as the masters of the sky. If we can acquire knowledge, for it is power they say; they say that but I think underworld knowledge isn't power but it is what keeps us alive, hustling and fighting for our goals would be fruitful`.

-`Tell me guys, why are you here`?

Before they could respond he proceeded

-`Because you want to acquire knowledge, so that you could rise above your obstacles and achieve your dreams or goals, so looking at how my mom struggled to make life for us, I began developing skills from the knowledge I gained from her, I began having dreams, and my dreams were about rising above my obstacles, so that I could achieve my goals and have a better life for my mom...

One thing she worked hard to give me was education, for it is a key to success, I held on to it, I got A`s and my mom was always proud of me. A smile on her face was the one thing that kept me moving forward. Looking at her bare feet made my heart soar, so I worked very hard at my primary level, high school and tertiary levels. She was the only one who would give me a warm hug when I had done well. No matter the family I came from, myself esteem was very high because of her...

On weekends I would take a spade and go gardening, she would seat on the stoop and watch me while gardening, her jokes kept me lifted. I remember this one time, it was Saturday afternoon and I was gardening and she started after one Nigerian who was selling some brooms stopped by selling, after he left my mom giggled; *"you know these Makoerekoere (Nigerians), they say they are ghosts!"* I stopped what I was doing and gave her all my attention, she went on; *"they say there was an incident whereby this Nigerian married a Mosotho woman, every time when the wife asked her husband to take her meet his family in Nigeria he would refuse. They bore two children, a boy and a girl, and after this, the woman insisted on going to Nigeria until the man gave in. They went there and when they approach one village in Nigeria, the man said; wait for me here, I will go to that house, pointing to one house in the village, that's my home, I will go warn them so that I don't surprise them...*

*She agreed and the husband went, time passed by, it was beginning to be very late and the woman began to be frustrated, she took the kids with her to the house he saw the husband get in...* I was listening attentively, she was so good in reciting stories, when telling me this she was serious and even imitating the woman when taking kids and her bags to the house, she went on; *when she got to the house, she introduced herself as `Manthabiseng from Lesotho, "I came here with Mr Jeff, it has* *been time since he got to this house but not getting back to us"* those in the house were surprised and confused, looked at each other, one woman said *"the person you are talking about died ten years ago"* they even took her to his grave, the woman fainted on the spot... at that time my mom started laughing and saying; *I told you, all of them are ghosts".*

I couldn't stop myself from laughing, I didn't even went on with gardening; I was so tired from laughter. I loved her with all my heart and for that I made sure that I don't disappoint her in my studies, she was so proud of me such that she didn't even notice her struggles.

-'Life is not for us but for the maker, we are the tools to battle the challenges that come with life. It is unpredictable, today you live happily, and tomorrow you are in the midst of problems. Today you are healthy, tomorrow you are ill, today you are alive and tomorrow you are dead. So be thankful for the life you are having today. Someone is probably at the brink of death lying in the hospital begging God to have the opportunity you are having right now, so use it wisely.

-`I could see my mom's life was deteriorating each day but she was a strong woman, she would still go out and perform her daily choirs.

Ladies and gentleman I just remembered when talking about choirs, I have one today, I have a meeting after lunch with some friends in town. Can we proceed tomorrow please?

'Why can't you postpone the meeting prof? Thabo protested, they all laughed and thanked prof for his time. Before they could leave, prof phoned Maria to be in his office and within seconds she was in.

Prof- `is my meeting still on with Mr Justice and Mr Emm, I am really looking forward to meeting those gentlemen`. Maria said yes;

Prof- `well, in that case, go with these peers of yours to grab some lunch, use this card to swipe` he handed her ATM card, `I will be on my way shortly`. Maria and Thabo's friends patted ways with prof, he took some papers from his briefcase and went to meet his friends. The meeting was to convene at 2pm at Lesotho sun hotel, now called Avani hotel. As he drove to the town prof was smiling from ear to ear as he kept thinking how much he missed his friends.

It has been a complete four years now without meeting because of professional duties, they most of the time travelled the world and hence there was no time for them at all to meet, this was a very special meeting for them. These peers met while they were doing their first year at the National University of Lesotho, they both enrolled in social work profession, they clicked a few days during their registration at school. Emm from Qacha, Justice from Thaba-bosiu Ha Seeiso and TP from Ngopets'oeu became friends from first year to fourth year, they have been studying together and almost every time they spend together, and this probably was because of their common background and their will to achieve that which they really wanted.

Their varsity life was fantastic, enjoyed spending time together and like other kids at varsity they would party and enjoy themselves but when it comes to books and attending classes they wouldn't miss a thing. Hence this had put them to being the best performers in their classes from first year until they completed their varsity. They became very active in community services. It was and still part of social work students in some courses to partake their knowledge to the communities, for these big three, it was in their nature to extend a helping hand, they were active members of the social workers association at the University, serving in the executive committee had let them to directing decision making into productive community services.

Among other things they did at the community levels was giving out used clothes to the needy, provision of psycho social support to the elderly and people living with disabilities and orphans and vulnerable children. Prof`s thinking and imaginations were nice such that the long journey became very short, he didn't even realise that he got to town just in few minutes.

Up the mountain, Prof Drove to Lesotho sun in winter afternoon, the weather wasn't good, it began dropping some showers of rain. As love of friends collided at the corridors, three friends met after a very long time. Nothing humbles a soul than the love one get from true friends, those guys who have been with you in times of joy and in times of tears. The warm breeze from the hotels air cons gave the big three the warmest welcome. For about five minutes they just set on the table without a word, only smiles on their faces said it all. Their table was right near the window, so they could see the world outside; they let their thinking transient the waves of the coldest breeze outside and deep down the thought about when they were young and energetic, battling the ground and fighting the obstacles of life were flowing in their brains.

The big three were professors, all of them in the field of social work, the profession they gave their all to making sure that it came to what it is today. Justice broke the silence like always; he started laughing non-stop; Kwa, Kwa, Kwa!

Prof TP- "hah, hah, hah, hah, you man! you still hold this horrible laughter even to date?"

They used to accuse him of having a horrific laughter, he would laugh aloud, opening his mouth wide while clapping his hands and stepping his feet at the same time. They followed suede, they laughed till their stomachs became painful. Emm still playing goody, goody;

Emm, "remember your positions now guys, you are professors"

He was at the time imitating professor Virus from three idiots. The meeting was very nice; they embarked on their carriers and the obstacles or challenges they were facing as a country in the field of social work and then their families in general. They say; work hard while young, retire at a very young age and enjoy your old age peacefully with no regrets. The big three lived their lives to the maximum while young. It was their time to enjoy.

Time flies when having fun but delay when you are having bad moments. Only the lights from the hotel could tell that it was very late, and yah! They had to part ways. They promised each other that at the end of every third month, they would come to the same hotel, on the same spot to grab some cup of tea. It was a promise they intended to keep and they kept it during their life time. They parted ways and everyone went on to his family.

## Summary of chapter 3

Chapter three professor talks to these three folks being Thabo, Retha and Lineo about his difficult life after varsity, his mother dies after a long illness. He gets piece jobs but he does not see progress in life. He tells them about the government that governed during his time that it wasn't good at all. At the end of the chapter he tries to show them that life after varsity is hard and requires a hustler as there is lack of job opportunities within the country.

## Chapter 3

Another day came without hesitating, yesterday was a special day, prof asked himself what that day holds for him, he thought; if yesterday was perfect, and then today should too. In the book of the secret it`s stated; "if you think positively then you will get positive results and the negatives likewise". The weather was clear that day, a sweet smell of a wet ground made the day even better. Prof was looking forward to meeting the young souls he recently made friends with. And like other days, he found them already waiting for him in the office.

They were patiently waiting for him to pick where they left yesterday. Their ears were ready for more interesting stories; they started first by telling prof how good was their lunch yesterday. They said they had a great day, blessed themselves with some fat cakes, chips and drink. Prof laughed lightly and said he was glad that they enjoyed, adding that he used to go for junk too while he was still a student.

Prof- `so guys, let us get down to business, but first I must say, my yesterday was wonderful too, if it was like a tape, I would rewind it and show you how much I enjoyed being with my friends, it was a very wonderful day of my life`.

-`after varsity, life became complicated on my side, you know at school we used to earn something at the end of the month, the little we got, I was able to assist my mom to go visit clinic for check-ups, for groceries and clothes for my younger brother`s child `Tlotlisang`; oh! I almost forgot, as time went on, my younger bro impregnated one girl in a nearby village, as a result she was forced to marry but within no time the wife left the child and disappeared. So since my mom wasn't able to support the family at all, I had to take care of them.

In times of happiness never forget your family because they were always there for you; never forget the people who supported you to being the person you are today, those who were there when everyone left you and that's your family, they were there when life had put you into shit, they were and will always be there to clean up your mess. So my family was my priority. I invested all I had to them because I knew my education came at the expenses of their emotional and physical happiness, just for me to achieve my goals...

We make plans of what we want to do after varsity or college, not knowing what the future holds for us, it is one secret that God kept from all of us, we plan and dream and many of our plans and dreams don't even see the day light, but because of the desire to change the situations around us, we keep on planning, dreaming and hustling forward. Life isn't easy after school, many don't have luck of getting a job right after completion and I was in that group which unluckily had nothing to do after varsity. Our system at the time was completely corrupt. Politicians chowed the country`s resources like food, youth unemployment was a disaster, crime rate high, divorce rate high, HIV/AIDS, school drop outs, teenage pregnancies, you name them, everything was high, and the people were also high due to high consumption of alcohol and drugs.

-`I began to swim in the midst of graduates unemployment, but hope was still there that one day I would sail through, a great spark was still kindling in my heart, and I told myself I would never give up, for I was born in the family of hustlers hence I had to hustle forward. I would get a daily, weekly or a monthly piece job and life went on, the little I got made some changes in my mom's life, she would go for check-ups and had something to eat...

Like I said everything escalated at the time, even my mom`s illness got worse, i tried all my best but the battle seemed to be battling me, the following years just after completing my varsity, I lost the fight. It was God`s work, I wouldn't have changed it, she was the apple of my eye and I was hers. I remember when she was in deep pain lying on the bed, she spoke with a shaky voice *"lord am I going to die and leave my children behind"*, her words touched my heart, as tears rolled down her cheeks she said; *"I wonder where I would be if it wasn't for you my child",* then deep in my heart I wondered too, where would I be if it wasn't for her, I couldn't control tears in my eyes, so I let them roll down my face...

At the time prof looked up, everyone could see he was trying to control tears that escaped his eyes, Rethabile and the other girl couldn't control their tears too so they let them roll.

"No one wants to die. Even people who want to go to heaven don't want to die to get there. And yet death is the destination we all share. No one has ever escaped it. And that is life's change agent. It clears out the old to make way for the new"- *Steve Jobs*

Prof wanted to take out the pain in his heart, so he proceeded- `they say time heals but for me! It still feels like yesterday. I thought after my graduation I would be able to help my mom,  so that she could rest and enjoy my salary peacefully like other women, enjoy the fruits of her perspiration, but it seemed I was just joking with myself, time and dates are only known by God`.

"They say that, when you are about to die, your life flashes before your eyes. They never tell you that when you watch someone you once loved dying, hovering between this life and the next, it`s twice as painful, because you`re reliving two lives that travelled one road together"- *Becca Fitzpatrick*

-`on your way to a target goal, you will experience pain, pain from losing the loved ones, but never give up, friends will leave you, but never five up, family members will look at you like you are a stranger, but never give up, you will experience failure and disappointments, but never ever give up, you will be powerless, lose your strength and lose all your energy, but never give up. If hope is still there, then the fire in your heart will never extinguish. Never give up.

After the darkest nights, the sun always rises. After the blackest nights, the sun will always rise!

-`Each obstacle leads you closer to your goal, and every disappointment, turn it to courage and a will to move forward. Many people after losing their loved ones take a long time than they should to mourn their loss. I cry not because of the pain but because of the life that I hope could have been, the life I imagined having with my mother and others who left me, this is the thinking that helped the fire in me to keep on burning, because the desire and the will to be somebody that matters in life was far greater than the past'.

Prof asked a rhetoric question unexpectedly;

-`do you matter?

-`You see, many people fail to achieve their goals because they are not sure whether they matter or not, or whether their dreams will bring good or destruction to themselves or their world. Some are very scared of their dreams such that they are unable to talk to others about them; they feel they might just be dismissed because they are not good to see the light of the day. Know that, if it scares you, then it is the sign that you should go for it, change this rotten and corrupt world. Know that, this world is not for the weak and if you are not willing to die for it-then you are not yet ready to go for it. Remember, you are the master of your own mind, you are the master of your own dreams, that's why it is you and you alone that will perfect it`.

The young girls and a boy came to professor`s office to listen, understand and make choices about their lives. You see when someone is talking life, sometimes you feel like you are not doing enough to change your own life, you feel like you are not doing enough to change your life, you feel like you are far back, such that it would be impossible to achieve your dreams. And many people let go brilliant ideas assuming that they might not work out, professor brought light to them and they felt like just going right away to fulfil their dreams.

-`you are you and the key to unlocking your own mind is you, no one can describe you better than yourself, life isn't a competition, live your own life, let your friends live theirs. Sure you still remember where I come from, I was born in that place alone and I will eventually part this world alone, its true we live side by side with others and sometimes we are bond together with them by blood, or friendship, but always remember, you are you, you have a purpose and your main purpose is to achieve your dreams`.

At that point prof was talking like a father, a motivational speaker, an educator, a teacher and yes a professor. He was instilling something that most young adults fail to understand, their purpose into this world.

Prof- `you asked me about my biography and I tried to highlight some of the things I came across in life, because all that I experienced is what has put me to the position I am in today. Every obstacle I encountered became a skill and experience to heading to the person I am today, life isn't easy I must admit, many fail to admit that because they deny the fact that, life is real. If you belief and hold on to that, you will see the reality in front of you, and you will get to choose between the right and the wrong and whatever you choose, make sure it leads you to the path that head to your desired goal.

-The hustler`s story never die-

Every employer needs a skilled employee, at least a year to five years of experience, that's what every work post says. After graduation you have nothing, except for the four years of theoretical knowledge you have been fed, lucky are social workers and other programs/professions that allow students to take lots of practical courses while still at school. Though not that much, but it does contribute much in building some work experience. It is then after being employed by high unemployment rate in the country you will have to start hustling for your life, some even engage in criminal activities so as to satisfy their needs, while others engage in promiscuous behaviours just to satisfy their needs sometimes.

It even hurts the most when young girls go to extend of opening up their legs for employers or people holding lucrative positions so they could offer them some jobs. Nothing hurts than seeing graduates moving up and down the street holding their CVs to apply for work knowing that they just apply for the sake of applying because the post (s) have already been allocated to those who are well connected, those who get a job even before it could be advertised.

## Summary of chapter 4

In this chapter prof tells Thabo, Lineo and Retha about the cruel system that ruled them at the time, people went on strike each week. As life got tough Justice his friend came to live with him and it is tough such that they don't even know what they eat papa with. He decides to put his certificates aside and hustle with his head, he get a job that does not satisfy him but he has no choice but to work for his Younger brother's child Tlotlisang as he took him and lived with him after his mother's death. The chapter ends with prof handing over his resignation letter to the manager at the work he was working at and headed home.

## Chapter 4

It was Wednesday, the other day, the morning seemed like meet day, and the streets were already filled up with people, yah! It had to, it was the 21$^{st}$ just after the 20$^{th}$ when some government officials like soldiers and police had just received their salaries, and everyone had something to spend. Even those who had nothing to fill up their car tanks were able to drive.

Professor was having a conversation in his mind as he was driving slowly to his office, yah like always he was looking forward to meeting his young friends and once they got to the office he started talking. At the time he was still standing, he had not even put his briefcase down or settled down properly;

Prof- `I was part of a cruel system, each month and each week people would go on strike for salary increase, police, wool and mohair farmers, teachers etc. went in a nation-wide strike, students from higher institutions fought for their monthly allowances, everything was just messed up. All what the people demanded was a good service delivery, but the government of that day closed its ears and we all suffered. At the time I had rented a room in town, this was to enable myself to rush to town without expenses whenever there was a post that required a social worker, but weeks, months and years passed by, nothing came to my rescue, I would negotiate to pay rent at the later dates in most months, luckily I had an understanding landlord...

Food was a problem too, I remember as time went on Justice, I hope you remember him, one of my friends, came to squat with me at my place so we could assist each other finding jobs, life wasn't easy at all. This one time we had nothing in the house but only papa so we were in dilemma on what we were to eat. We only had M2 so we debated whether to buy tea bag so that we could eat with tea, but there was no sugar unfortunately, we couldn't go to neighbours to beg for it because you know life in the Maseru/cities isn't that easy, it is the survival of the fittest there (every man for himself). We decided to let go the idea of tea bags and went for zimbas, you see this big chilli zimbas, we bought two packets and had our lunch, problem solved. Sometimes we would buy archer to it papa with it, and because we had that hope that one day things would change for better, we enjoyed eating and laughing at the same time saying; "one day will be one day…

It would sound like a lie when we tell this to our children" and yah! Today I am giving you the story of my own hustle, you don't have to hustle the same way I did so as to get to where I am, but my story to the right mind says that; you are not alone in this world, if faced with this many problems in life, know that, there are probably more people who are faced with even worse problems. Someone is busy battling those problems as we speak, so you are not alone and your story will never die if you want it not to; the hustlers story never die…

As months passed by I decided to put my qualifications aside and hustle with my brain, within no time I got a job in one big shop around town where I was earning some peanuts (little salary) at the end of the month, but you know what! I didn't care; all I cared about was to end up reaching my goals. the more I tried working hard was the more I suffered, after the passing of my mom, I had no choice but to take Tlotlisang so as to stay with him, he was about to complete his 4th year birthday, I had to take care of him, nurse him like a child, make sure he had clothes and eat properly.

Everything was just complicated for me but I had no other choice, back at home, I had to support my younger bro too as he had nothing too, he would have some piece job today and tomorrow gone. My life was just not so in a straight line. But then I had to contain myself, wake up early in the morning bath and hit the road, that was my daily routine, I felt like I was standing on one spot, just stationary, no progress in my life at all, and one day I just decided to quit my job, I didn't know what I was going to do after that, but I would always tell myself that, God was in control. I remember that day I set on the table, it was Tuesday evening after work; I set round my laptop and typed.

Ngope-ts`oeu hangaka

P. O Box 182

Roma 180

Maseru 100

24/11/2017

Human resource manager

P.O Box *****

********

Maseru 100

Dear sir/ Madam

<u>Re: Resignation</u>

I hereby inform you of my resignation as a fruits and verge assistant.

It has been a great pleasure working with you, thank you for the opportunity you granted me.

Yours faithfully

TP

The following morning I headed to the manager's office and handed him the letter.
Sometimes you should be willing to take risks, life without risks is boring;
remember, life is a risk by itself, you can wake up healthy in the morning, fell by the
bed side and boom!! Die, or walk just outside, trip and break a leg. So never be
afraid of taking risks because it is from changing that which we do daily that we are
to reap different results.

When you have done something good, your soul come to peace, your mind is set
tranquil, a sweet flow of your blood rush through your veins and your heart beat
once, twice and you feel alive after a long, long time. That's what I felt after handing
over my resignation letter, it was then I realised that, I have been burdening myself
for something I didn't like but for money so as to take care of my family and my
own basic needs. So my children; I know I might sound like I am reciting you a ferry
tail, but the truth be told, life out here isn't a play game. I know, school might be
boring now for you because of endless assignments, tests and presentations, but
being at school at the time was much better than being a graduate. Work hard at
school, graduate and after that never stop hustling.

Wednesday session was longer than other days, it was getting late, but separation
wasn't what they were looking forward to.

Prof- `ladies, gentleman, let us stop here for today, in few minutes the whole place
will be covered in darkness, we should head home`.

They all exchanged their goodbyes and parted ways. Since time wasn't on prof's
side too, he headed to his car and hit the road, people walked in numbers from
different angles. It was after work, everyone was going home, traffic germ gave him
a headache, but nothing could be done. In his mind he thought about life; seeing
everyone in hurry going home to their families, he imagined; life as a drama,
everyone has a particular role to play, you see in drama, there are players and there
are spectators. Player's main role is to play and entertain those watching, and the
spectator's roles are to laugh or cry if there is need...

Life is like that, everyone performs his/her role, but out there are those people who are just there to watch, and you find that their main task is to judge, lead others astray, or even take from the hard workers, its life, it`s just like a drama. Live each day to enjoy it, let moments of disappointments pass you by, let criticisms pass by the other ear, be confident in whatever role life chose for you, and aspire to be the best in the role you are playing.

Imaginations that took over prof`s mind made him not to even see that he was already at his gate, dinner was already served and the family was just waiting for him for just few minutes, fortunately he got in before they could lose their appetite. His wife came to welcome him with a hug, took his brief case and went to his office in the house to put it. His boy just smiled, they all set down to eat, and the night was going to be a long one for he was very tired.

## Summary of chapter 5

This chapter 'Makatleho didn't wake her husband Prof, she takes the child to school. Professor TP arrives late at work and finds his clients already in the office. He tells them about his life after quitting the job, but finds another job which made way to his good life. He tells them about grand father's story which became his inspiration to coming to where he was. He tells them he went on for the Masters degree as he wasn't feeling fine about just having a degree. The chapter ends describing the personality of professor TP.

## Chapter 5

The sun raises hit the room, and the light flashed in his eyes, woke him up, he wondered what was happening because he thought he just got in bed, only to find that it was early in the morning, 7am, his wife and the kid had already finished everything and were ready to leave.

Prof- "why didn't you wake me up `Matlotliso?"

`Matlotliso- "I tried and I lost, so I decided to let you rest, we are leaving, I will drive the other car and drop the kid to school"

She gave him a light kiss and parted. Prof woke up immediately and went to take a bath, the meal was readily made for him, so he couldn`t waste time he ate within a minute and headed to his car and hit the road, he was in hurry so that he wouldn't make his friends wait for him for a long period of time. Each day he was drawing closer to them, and they got attached to him like they were his blood children.

He got to the office after 9am, they had so long waited for him but they didn't even realise that because of Maria; she was a talkative lady who have some sense of humour, so they enjoyed hanging around with her too. They were glad to see prof as they said they were at the edge of giving up thinking he wasn't coming to work

Prof-"I am here, let`s get down to business, shall we?"

-Never ever quit on yourself-

If there is anyone on this world who knows better about you, then that person is you; every decision or choice that you take, it is up to you whether it will hurt you or make you brave, life is hard, so hard such that when you sit down and think about it harder, it might scare the hell out of you. Even if it`s that hard, you sleep without roofs under your head, you sleep with an empty stomach, having no shoes on your feet; never give up on yourself. Remember it is you and you alone that can walk through the sea of your own problems and fight the way out of it.

After quitting my job, I had nothing and no one to help me, but hope was still in my heart, I could still see the light at the end of the tunnel, I knew that somewhere someday all my problems would just fade away and my future would be as white as snow on the beautiful mountains of the mountain kingdom of Lesotho. Before long I got a job and finally I got to implement my social work skills, though it was a short contract but I was able to see for once progress in my life, I could feet my family while investing a little for my future plans.

Having a degree is one achievement that to us who came from very impoverished families feels like having the whole world. You see, in my blood line I was the only one who managed to make it as far as the University; my grandfather managed to reach form E and he was somebody (boss like) in the mines in South Africa. You remember my grandfather for sure, the one I told you he died the same year I was born! When I heard about his life, I became fascinated, he became my role model because of his intelligence, hard work and the good heart he had.

I was told when he came home from South Africa especially during festive seasons, he would buy some groceries for the family, extended family members and even some neighbours. He was a very good man, an angel sent from above, but because the world is cruel and doesn't deserve good people, his friends murdered him. It is said that he was betrayed by his own brother being my father but killed by his own friends, the people he assisted in getting jobs as he was a foreman in one gold mine in SA. Having heard his stories, I wanted as a young man to follow his footsteps, he became dearly a role model, I wanted so bad to break his record, I was motivated by his story, though he died a horrible death, but his good deeds left a mark to our hearts we who believed in his good work...

So I was here; having a degree is such an honour, but honestly speaking, a degree nowadays is like a grade 12 certificate, everyone has it, everywhere you go you find degree holders, let alone when there is an employment post, hundreds and thousands of degree holders would even fight for one or two posts. I wanted so bad to get out of that competition, I felt like I was suffocating; you know when you are covered by a plastic bag or drowning in a pool of water! I just felt like I was running out of air. So I had to make a plan, invested in multiple businesses and I was able to make quick cash, ventured in a small printing business and made more money. My plan was to pay back the National Manpower Secretariat (NMDS) so that they could pay my fees.

As time went on, I was doing my master's degree in Social work; I wanted to step up the ladder until I reach my final destination`.

At the time prof was lifting his hands looking lightly into the thin air as he looks up the sky (the ceiling of cause) it was like he was seeing himself as he took step by step up the ladder, it was like he was looking into himself and marvelling at the road he travelled, or maybe watching a movie or video of his entire life into the air. They (girls and a boy) were silent, imagining themselves walking the same path, telling stories to others when they grow up, they didn't care about time, they didn't care whether to do group work at school or not, all they cared about was sitting beside professor and listen to him as he gave them knowledge in hands. The ups and downs he went through; he was a well-known professor, the world knew about him but no one cared much about approaching him, they thought he was arrogant as he wasn't a talkative man, that's why he was very happy when the young souls came to his office for guidance.

In fact, professor was a nice person, full of love for other people, that one man who would spend all he has to seeing the lives of other people change, he was the helper, a loving type, and a type of a person you would always want to be with. That's professor for you.

They were still enjoying imaginations of their minds when prof warn them;

Pro-`ladies and gentleman, go study it`s already late, let us meet again tomorrow, same time, same place`.

## Summary of Chapter 6

In this chapter prof talks about the road to success and tells his clients that hard work and dedication to what they do is key to everything important in the world. And this is the last day of prof and his clients, they part ways though they didn't expect that so soon as they are having great time with prof, thank him for his time and part ways.

## Chapter 6

We are told in the book of Genesis that; in the beginning, there was no light, only darkness, earth and water were mixed, and therefore, no plants or any life could have lived. God came and everything was put in its place, darkness faded, light came, plants and animals of every kind were given breath and everything got shaped and put in order.

Life by itself has no order nor meaning, but we his people, the persons of the creator, are tasked with the duty of giving order to our lives and it seems therefore; it is in our hands to either destroy or build our future, through the dreams and goals we set, we give order to our lives because at least we set a deadline, for we say, we want to live up to that far, we want to achieve that at one point in time, and that, that`s what give our lives a meaning.

Thursday, outside everything could be seen was alive, though grass wasn't green, everything was blurry, voices of happy people could be heard from the outside. Everyone was already moving up and down the street, doing what they do day by day. Prof woke up feeling very energetic. Looking forward to meeting his friends, it was now four days since he met them, but it felt like they had known each other for about four years now. They have that connection that felt like they were age mates.

He made preparations very fast and headed to his office, it was really a wonderful Thursday, like the other days he found them already in the office waiting for him so he didn't waste time…

Prof-`everyone in life has a compass and this compasses are the ones that guide us to achieving what we really want in life, you have that inner voice that will tell you what is right and what is wrong. Us Basotho before we decide whether to do something or not, we would be saying "ke pelo li peli" (I have too hearts), `the one says do it while the other says don't`, then we would go with the one which has more weight than the other.

At your age I know you have friends, some might be good while others might be bad influencers; it is up to you to follow your own compass, not that of your friend, what your friends intend to achieve in the end has nothing to do with you, for you have your own goals too. If your friend`s compass says they should head north; follow your own because it might be saying you should head south. Do not fall a victim of your friend`s dreams.

I chose my own path, though we were that close with my friends, everyone followed his own heart, I returned to school to do my Masters and they did too, I was full time, they were part time, on top of what I was doing, I became very interested in businesses and investments and I was very successful in what I was doing, but that, that wasn't my dream, that was a means of earning some extra income. To find my true dream I had to follow my heart and my heart gave me what I wanted and what I had always cried for, and this was to change the world because I believed that; "Even just a drop of rain contributes in making a beautiful waterfall" and the only way I could touch the souls around the world was through writing, this was my true passion and I had to follow it.

-`The road to success`-

It is such a narrow path to success, and not all of us shall reach where we hope to go, but we all work hard to reach the Promised Land. Sometimes it might feel like you are there while to other people you seem not to even have started, but because that which you dream is known only by you, it`s only you who can tell whether you have succeeded or not. Success is reaching that which you wished to have achieved.

Through struggles, hard work and hustle you get it, others just get lucky, hit the jackpot, boom! They get to their destination. Success is immeasurable; no one can know whether you are successful except yourself. I can`t say I am successful now, yah! To some point I am because I have reached most of my goals but there are some I haven't, then after achieving them, its then I can tell a better story.

I told you my passion is writing; while I was at varsity level doing my degree I used to write short scripts on motivation, but because I had no money to publish, I just wrote because I loved, I even went to an extent of self-publishing my first script on Amazon. It was my first writing which I named "Unemployment is an illusion", because I had no cash to promote it, it was just there and no one was able to access it. But you know what! I didn't give up because I believed in writing, hence I just wrote and wrote without giving a damn whether to publish or not.

I then wrote another script which I named "The journal of Social work', this was specifically meant for social workers both students and practitioners and I send it to many social work groups in the country, I just didn't care whether I get paid or not I just followed my passion, so you see! It is such a good thing to follow your heart, do that thing which you feel after doing it your heart would be at ease and your soul would be satisfied. Remember; life is not a competition, everyone is running his own race, everyone is following his own compass, so just keep following yours, for that that is where your future lays.

Prof-'look outside the window and see, the trees shaded their leaves, the grass is brownish, no life, rivers begin to run try, everything seem to be dead. But we all know that they are all this way because of winter, because of the cold. Deep inside us we know that, that which seems like the end only marks the beginning, summer would soon come, and all that which was presumed dead would come to life again. They will bear fruits, grass would have seedlings and rivers would overflow with water again.

Winter and summer symbolises exactly what we go through in life, today might be dark, but tomorrow the sun rise again, today you might be drowning in problems but tomorrow you sail through. I said few days ago that; life without challenges is just boring. It wouldn't be life if there were no challenges/ problems, we wouldn't be able to truly know ourselves and others, for no one would extend a helping hand to the other. There would be no education systems, no shops, public transport, nothing at all because no one would be in need of the services of the other.

Everything we see which is important is meant to ease life; actually its main purpose is to eliminate a certain problem. Government; their duty is to address people's problems, supermarkets; to curb unemployment, provide food etc. and for owners to make money, education on the other hand help you to battle your problems or cope well with them. Then imagine life without problems; it wouldn't be interesting at all.

For you to get anything you want in this life, you should sweat, get off your comfort zone and hustle. Some of you are still lucky you have parents, who are working and are supportive to you, but not many still has them, they have to work hard to get their daily bread for themselves and their families.

-`hard work and discipline`-

If it wasn't for my hard work, I wouldn't be here talking to you, I wouldn't have been the world known professor and entrepreneur, because I worked hard to get to where I am today. It seems like a just a straight path from where you are to where I am; I am saying this because some years ago, I was a student like you, I was just ambitious like you are; you know what! I didn't stop, nothing stopped me, and I sailed through my problems and got my medal.

Discipline is crucial to every door of success, when we start our conversation few days ago; I talked about knowing your foundation, because there is where discipline lies. Every parent raises their children to be such respectful and disciplined kids, many who engage in unacceptable behaviours have often forgotten their foundations, therefore the roots of their psychological wellbeing is deteriorated hence leading them to unpleasant behaviours.

It has been an honour talking to you my children; this marks my final words in our conversation, and tomorrow is Friday. I know you young folks; no one can stop you when it`s Friday; you want to go out and chill with friends.

They were all in smiles when he was saying that, but deep inside, they were very upset and emotional as they had to partway with their friend, it was already late so everyone headed home including professor.

## Summary of Part 2 and chapters 7 to 13

Part 2 of this book shows that everything that went on in Part 1 was just a dream that TP was telling his friends, actually they were in the cave when he was telling them the story of him as a professor, and he tells them why he is a professor in that dream. He is saying this as they freeze in a cave, the snow is about to cover the whole cave and they are freezing, most chapters starts with the end and end with the start. Before they reach the cave they had organised a group of people who specialised in different disciplines to combine brains so as to topple the dictatorship government which was ruling at the time. They create a system that is very sophisticated and they have spy and informants in all government agencies. They find themselves running from time to time and the people closer to them get hurt most of the time.

Main characters in all the chapters are TP, the master mind behind web of toppling the government, Emm and Justice are friends to TP and together they are the big three who are willing to give up their lives to remove the government.

## Summary of chapter 7

The chapter starts with TP telling his friends Emm and Justice about his dream as a professor and how come he chose the professor tittle. We see the name KB which is one of TP's friends who gave him a marijuana seed and this name came up as he tries to make sense to Emm and Justice why he is a professor in a dream. They organise a team to topple the government, and it is made up of psychologists, economists, social workers, IT specialists etc. And it ends by showing that IT specialists are made up of those coming from the Military Intelligence (MI) of the country and the National Security Services (NSS).

## PART 2

# Chapter 7

## Dream .......why professor?

You can call it a fantasy or a day dream, but nothing so good and wonderful than dreaming about the things you want to achieve. The goals you set yourself and you could see them very far away, but in your head you are already living them, seeing yourself in that beautiful car, and living happily in your house with your family. All these put a smile on your face. It`s such a positive energy that keep you moving forward and that energy leads you to that dream that you can`t stop it from playing and replaying in your mind.

"Have you ever tried to narrate your goal to someone and they don't understand you? They think you are nuts. Yeah! It happens; there is one this friend who is a big dreamer, and some of the things he dream sound like they are out of this world. His mom doesn't even like listening to him, but somehow it feels fantastic when listening attentively to what he would be saying, and he is an amazing man because he is a dreamer like me. We move along a similar path, so our language match and the way we do things is such entertaining, we enjoy dreaming and hustling hard so that one day we get to our final destination.

You see its okay if they don't get your point, if they don't understand you at all, it`s just okay to be abnormal, never stop dreaming because nothing sweet than living the future of your own imaginations.

Let me tell you something you don't know about me; I am a dreamer;

TP was all smiles as he narrates his story to his friends Emm and Justice; "guys don't you see through my brains, because I can see through yours, that you are wondering; who is professor actually? Well! Let me tell you; I am the professor in my dream. I am working hard to fulfil my prophesy, the story in my head play each day repeatedly, and my blood flow very fast, something sweat flows with it, my mind transcends  its bonds and I can live my dream while awake, in my sleep, and verbally I can say it.

Some call me a lunar but I don't care, because people are made to talk, I just follow my mind. Some say I think too much and yah, I have to for my mind is created to think". He was deeply emotional when talking to his friends for he knew they were the only ones who could understand what he was saying; well! Even if they couldn't understand but they would nod their heads like they understood. That's what friends are for right? When you talk nonsense but emotional they would pretend they understand so that you feel better, every one listened attentively without interrupting.

-"you would remember, I once got a marijuana seed from one of our friend, KB, when we were working for one company in the Mokhotlong district; he used to smoke some dagga after hard work in the evening to stabilise his mind. Before we could finish that study we were doing, he ran out of marijuana, he didn't smoke any type of marijuana except cannabis, it was so special to him. Where he used to put his dagga was one seed, just one! He gave it to me, I made small plot where I rented a house in Maseru, and so I put the seed in the soil and watered it daily.

After some weeks it grew, I was motivated to see it growing and bearing some seeds too, so I kept watering it; I was fascinated by its greenness and I thought, if life was as green as this marijuana, I guess we would be very happy people. I kept watering it until it made the seeds. It was so beautiful and motivating, it triggered so many ideas in my mind. I thought, if we could be given a chance to grow this in our country, we would change to better as a nation...and because of this you (Justice and Emm) named me professor. You named me a thinker, someone who could think outside the box to live a better life, yes that is where the name Prof came fro m".

-"guys life isn't just about waking up in the morning, eating and sleeping again, but it's about thinking, dreaming and getting off bed to follow your dreams. If you are a dreamer like me, follow me; in my dream I told you about young persons who wanted to learn about my life as a professor, they came to my office (yes in my dream) because they dreamed and they thought; 'the only way to achieve our dreams is to find or go to someone who has gone through this path, so we follow him'.

Winston Churchill once said "I have met my enemy and my enemy is me". The only person who will stop you from going for what you want is you, the deepest negative energy inside you is your enemy and the only way to defeat your enemy is to face it. A dream is a smooth thinking that has no obstacles ahead of it. But the obstacles we create in our heads are the ones that stop us from achieving it. Obstacles are in the head I reiterate; dreams or goals are also in the head, hence the only way to get to your goals is to use your head and defeat the monsters in it.

TP was looking at his friends' one by one, eye to an eye and it could be spotted that everyone was deeply digesting their lives, goals and the mess they were in.

Talking about mess; earlier that morning the boys were ready to evacuate their office after realising that they have been spotted. They were not sure who hacked their system yet, but they had to take all they have got and flee to the mountains. There was no proper shelter but they found a scary cave where they could settle. They had left their vehicle in one forest just below the mountains they were hiding in. they had cut few trees and bushes and put them on the vehicle to hide it.

It was now a year and a half since they have been in business, they had connections everywhere, their system was just a web of multidisciplinary young professionals willing to change the ruling system of the country, from head to the toe, from primary schools to universities, from one ministry to another, from village health workers to big hospitals, from security guards to soldiers (LDF [MI], NSS) police, police constables, inmates, bankers etc. They had everyone in place, their system was just impenetrable. On top of the chain was this big three, you wouldn't even think anything was going on around them as they were just normal people, who are known of good deeds, donate to charity organizations, provide psycho social support to those who needed it and try as much to help those who were in need.

Their motto was `to do GOOD no matter what` and yah, they were doing well for their own country, for everyone cried each day without doing anything. At first they had gathered all their friends, who specialised in different fields of studies. The meeting was called "The Hustlers", it was held in one house down town in Maseru; it was an abandoned house they knew no one would go there. As the meeting convene;

TP who chaired the meeting started;

-"we called you here today because of the brains, and in this brains we need the minds, to merge these minds to form something impenetrable, but that which can penetrate to every system and every sector of this country. We will not use force nor coercion but the mind to do what is right, but if there shall be a need for force, then we shall unleash it, we will not be part of it, we would just watch from a distance when they fight, and we will rebuild afterwards. The system governing us is corrupt to the core and it seems everyone is enjoying it, for no one wants to take a step to bring it down, so it`s just us, it`s either we do it now or never`.

Everyone was silent and nodding with their heads, it showed they understood and said... "We are in"

The group had IT specialists, doctors, political scientists, psychologists, social workers etc. so they could extend their connections to all government agencies. They hired a three roomed house meant for their work, there was a room for their equipment like computers and big display screens and few chairs, there was also a kitchen for refreshments, and the other room was a bed room for a security guard. Few CCTV cameras were installed outside the house, at the back, in front and at the gate. They had a 4*4 Toyota Hilux that they used to move around the country to gather information.

The first steps of their work was to gather information on politics and everything that they needed from local newspapers and their informants in their respective work places gave them a lot of information. Each day great work was done and piece of information they gathered day by day was so beneficial. They lay so low you wouldn't suspect a thing was going on with them. Like I said, confidentiality was one thing that had brought them together; they were like one big family. Each day everyone in the evening had to rush to the office to discuss some progress and where they needed to improve, they went step by step as they did not want to rush things to avoid mistakes.

About three IT specialists were working full time at the office, developing a web and complicated software that was hard to penetrate. One specialist was a former military intelligence officer (MI) others were from the National Security Service

(NSS) and lastly the other one was a product of the National University of Lesotho; he was unemployed. Everything was becoming successful each day. It is said that 'you should never let fear conquer your mind or dreams, for if you let it; you therefore let a false evidence that appears as though real to stop you from going where you want to go'. If Lesotho needed a change; then it needed great minds like the boys and girls who were willing to give up their lives to achieve the impossible.

At the moment, more information kept moving in, it was time for the next step…

## Summary of chapter 8

In this chapter, TP's team, they call themselves "the Hustlers" hacks the MI and NSS systems so as to expose the bad deeds of the two agencies and the government, they are afraid that things might get out of hands as they found months back that their information had been leaked by some members who accepted bribe so as to give up the agency. In this mission they want these agencies to fight themselves so that they end up toppling the government. As the hacking goes on they are tipped by their informant within the army that the army knows their where about, so they take whatever they have and run to the mountains, the weather is not good, hence they find themselves freezing in a cave as they head to one of TP's cattle posts in the Semonkong mountains.

## Chapter 8

"Optimism is a strategy for making a better future. Because unless you believe that the future can be better, it's unlikely you will step up and take responsibility for making it so. If you assume that there's no hope, you guarantee that there will be no hope. If you assume that there is an instinct for freedom, that there are opportunities to change things, there is a chance you may contribute to making a better world. The choice is yours". *– Noam Chomsky*

The next step was to hack few bank accounts and personal information of top officials of the country, make connections on how they get the money, and if they are found dirty; leak the information; this mission had to be handled with care and the presence of everyone that day had to be visible. They were to work the whole night as this was a crucial stage.  It is true it wasn't going to be a one day mission, but they wanted to be sure if the first steps succeeds or fails, and if it fails then they would be there to witness and run if possible, for it would mean they are in trouble.

Everyone was sweating; fortunately they managed to hack few personal accounts and computers of the officials and leaked the information to social media (face book, twitter, WhatsApp etc.) and they enjoyed watching. This first stage assured them that their system was much sophisticated and for months that came by, they were the eye openers of the people. Their connections grew day by day, such that even the advisor or the closest man besides the prime minister was part of their web.

The second mission was to hack NSS and MI systems. They say 'life is a risk by itself, so why not take a risk anyway?' after this mission, things wouldn't be as they were, things were to change automatically, their lives would be in danger, they would have to surrender, be killed or run for their lives.

It was completely a year since planning and some of the implementation parts were completed, this was a very sensitive mission that would be handled carefully. It`s true that; "too many people spoil the broths". TP had been running a monthly secret spy mission on his work mates in every sector, only two people knew about the mission, Emm and Justice; this was to ensure that confidentiality was kept, that they do not get killed or attacked while asleep. They had secret phones that they used to communicate with their spy. and they had found out that some of the information about their whereabouts and their operation could be leaked at any moment; this was due to some disagreements that occurred months back in the office.

It seemed some members of the crew had been bribed to give up the web, this was revealed by TP's spy that the fire was starting to burn. NSS and MI had collaborated forces to find "the Hustlers" this is why the mission they were about to embark on was called secretively; all members didn't get any calls like they always do. But a 4*4 Hilux worked non-stop that night, picking members while sleeping and delivering them to another office, different from the usual one, no one knew about it except the big three.

The office had been in place from the scratch. It was mainly meant to spy "the Hustlers", only two people worked in the office except the spy field workers who came once or twice to the office; they were highly trained specialists who do love their work with all their hearts. No one was paid here. Except the IT specialists because they didn't leave the office, they were paid in cash; no electronic transfers.

After picking all the informants, they were made aware of the mission they were about to get into. Everyone had to give away their phone or any electronic devise.

TP-"There are some of you who have leaked some of our important information; we didn't expect this from you, we trusted each other with all our hearts, but it seems, we have not been fighting for one goal after all this time. But then, it's okay because after this night I will stand on top of Thabana-ntlenyana (the highest/tallest mountain in Lesotho) and watch as this night's mission take place, I will smile, and the coming generations will mark this day as the day of their liberation. Some of us were trained to hold a pen and a paper; to use a brain to fight guns, and other war machines;

today let the world know that; it is through the mind that we have the bread on the table, a gun in the hand and the form of government we have today, it creates, it destroys, we chose this path, it would be a waste of time if we worked this much and just give up when we are about to complete our final mission. Remember; Nelson Mandela once said; 'winners are those who never give up'; we made mistakes as the group, as the nation, it is therefore our responsibility to clean our own mess".

No one said anything; the team was just speechless, motionless, they were only waiting for orders to get to work.

TP- "let's get down to work, our mission like I said earlier, is to hack the MI systems, hack NSS systems, I had they joined forces, we hit them where they are not expecting; only sensitive information, if there is any possibilities that MI or NSS has said or did anything bad about or to the other, lets expose them to the other's system; let us see where the weakness of our prime minister and his government is and expose them to their systems, let them divide, expose the bad deeds of the commander and his subordinates, let there be two factions. Military would fight itself; and they would fight the NSS on the other hand.

Since the commander already hate the prime minister according to our findings, the large faction that follows the general will follow him to attack state house. We have to hack cell phone towers, command the soldiers guarding prime minister and other officials to return to the barracks with immediate effect. Listen to every words exchanged within the state house; no calls in or out; guys, it's our time, let the shows begin.

IT specialists were already doing their work at the time, many were becoming frustrated, fear on their faces could be spotted, but no one actually gave a damn; they were in this and there was no turning back; perspiration on their foreheads, silence overwhelmed the room, only few local radio stations were playing; click, click, click sounds from computer key boards could be heard, all eyes on the big screen; they could see within the MI, NSS and state house for they had long installed their micro cameras, they could see frustrated faces of IT specialists within the agencies as they try to figure what was happening to their own systems.

Their systems started to germ, few minutes "the Hustlers" made them to go dark and they rebooted again with a mokorotlo sign on the screens and the message that went like "if it takes my life to fight for my beloved country, so be it". After this "the Hustlers" started leaking out the information on their computer screens, panic and frustration could be seen on the other side. The only thing that was to happen was for the commander to give orders, it was becoming ugly, they were all accusing one another, insults started to be exchanged between the MI and NSS. The next step was to release the information regarding the military personnel and the state house. It was becoming ugly and entertaining at the same time. The night was too short, they knew when the sun rises and darkness fades, the country would be a war zone, but their mission would be completed with soldiers temporarily taking the prime minister`s office.

Time moved fast, tension in two top offices (MI & NSS) started being visible, radio stations went off... they knew that soldiers probably did that; at least they were working at "the Hustlers" favour unknowingly! Their duty now was to shut down the cell phone towers and within no time they were shut, and recalled the prime minister`s guards to the barracks, he was beginning to be afraid of what was going on, but nothing he could do...darkness started fading away but at least winter nights are much longer than summers, it gave them time to complete their mission; everything was getting out of hands, military vehicles were spotted everywhere in the streets, more troops kept being deployed around town.

The faxes that they kept being received from other districts said the situation was getting out of hands. All faxes were read by only two people for confidentiality purposes and to minimise frustration on members; the one that captured their eyes was the one which said "they know, you need to hit the road now, and I mean now!" it was coming from trusted informants who were IT specialists in the military, so it was without any doubt that things were beginning to backfire.

They didn't know how come they were busted but they knew that something like this would happen anytime since their information had been leaked by some members little by little in the past few months, but then; every escape plan was put in place, precaution measures were to be followed for everyone to be safe. They had an agreement that, if a member (s) gets arrested, they shouldn't give up other members at any cost so that they could assist them with paying bails and use their connections to get them out.

The office had a long tunnel, that lead the way outside town and the tunnel had two other branches, the first one was heading North where all team members would have to run for their lives and the other one was heading west side where the vehicle was already there; they left it yesterday while delivering all the members to the office. The big three to the west side branch of the tunnel and got to the vehicle and hit the road.

All the hard drives were taken and other important documents while all left information was destroyed and everything that could provide a lead to their where about had to be destroyed. There were few vehicles in the street since the fleet of military vehicles had occupied most roads and because people were afraid of all that was going on.

The day was cloudy and light rain was beginning to fall, cold breeze was also woofing in the space, silence in the car could be heard by the deaf; but then they had to flee; flee in to the deepest mountains of the mountain Kingdome. To break the silence TP played a music by an artist called Moja-lihloho saying "thota khutsufala" (shorten the way). They were heading to Semonkong; they already had a shelter to hide for a few days. This was one of TP's few places where he was rearing his sheep and goats. He hit the accelerator up the mountains and the mountains were beginning to be invisible due to clouds, rain began to pour cats and dogs.

It was said by the Lesotho meteorological services that snow fall should be expected that day and as they reach the mountains, the snow had started falling like cut papers. They didn't care much of what was going on where they came from, they only cared about their lives. The road was beginning to be hard to drive, but then they had to reach the mountains. They were already moving in the gravel roads of Semokong, very far somewhere they drove even where there were no roads, no nearby villages could be spotted because of snow; only TP knew about this place, his friends only heard from him when they were discussing their plans; unfortunately their plan didn't cater for snow for each one of them only had a blanked and a freezer suit but they had no matches/lighter as everything was at the place they were heading. So there they were in the cave!!!...

## Summary of chapter 9

Characters are TP, Emm, Justice, and Katleho (TP's younger brother). TP, Emm and Justice are in the cave they got in after escaping, snow fall harder and they are freezing. They pass out in the cave due to cold; they find themselves in a house roofed with thatch when they wake. Apparently they were rescued by Katleho and his friend, Katleho tells them it is the third day since they passed out, and TP remembers that he once told Katleho to go find them there as they had important mission to fulfill and that might cause them to run, so he would find them there to help them with their things. The chapter ends with these three friends deciding to lie law for a month without phones and other devices that might lead to their where abouts.

## Chapter 9

Returning to the vehicle would be a risk too, the cold from snow would paralyse them, so they decided to stay; it was beginning to be late, it wasn't that late but because of snow and clouds and the mountains that surrounded them, darkness began falling each minute. TP knew by that cave they were in, that they were not very far from where they were going.

TP-"two hours at least"

-"Two hours!?" with surprised faces Emm and Justice asked

TP-"Yah two hours"

He was looking up the cave when he says; "so guys the story of my professorship is the story I am hoping to achieve one day; one day after all this mess, we would fulfil our dreams, at least we fought for the coming generations, though not knowing what is really going on where we just come from, but I can assure you that, after today, this country would be a different one; where would it be without us?

The snow was going higher and higher such that in few hours it would be hard to see outside the cave, the cold began penetrating their bones and they began to freeze, but they didn't give up.

TP- "life is a fight guys, if you are not willing to fight; nothing you will get, lets hang in there, everything will just be fine",

Their mouths ran try, voices tremble with cold as they spoke. But they had smiles on their faces.

TP- "If I die today, I will die a happy man, knowing that I didn't just seat on my back when my people were denied what is rightfully theirs, and my soul will be much happier and rejoice in heaven".

They began not to feel their feet, even their hands were becoming numb, eyes began closing; they knew they had come to the end of their journey. The two had already closed their eyes, so TP let his close too...

...

"Strange is our situation here upon earth. Each of us cones short visit, not knowing why, yet sometimes seeming to divine a purpose. From the standpoint of daily life, however, there is one thing we do know – that man is here for the sake of other men." – *Albert Einstein*

There was a fire place in the middle of the room, very big stones were the ones that had built the house; he opened his eyes but everything was just blurry, the house seemed like it was roofed with thatch, for about thirty minutes, he was trying to find himself and where he was and how he got there. Nothing made sense; he could hear voices outside, sounds of sheep, goats and dogs burking, he wasn't sure where he really was.

Beside him were his friends who just woke up and were also trying to digest everything but for over an hour they didn't get any answer. Just when they were asking themselves endless questions, someone entered the room. It was Katleho; they recognised him immediately (you remember the younger brother of TP right?). They regained their senses; he was the one who found the big three in the cave.

TP (recalling) *"One day after all this we would have to run to the mountains, be prepared for us, prepare everything that we are to use in a period of a month; come lets go; I want to show you something, on the 24th august we have a very important and sensitive mission to take, and after that we would have nothing to do but to flee, for military and NSS and police would be on  our tail, you see this cave; we would rest in it before we travel to the post, come to the cave in the evening so that you would help us carry some of our stuff'.*

TP was remembering, it was him with Katleho in a secret meeting they held at the cave few months back. Katleho explained how he found the cave covered with snow but with the help of his friend who is also a child's uncle were able to remove the snow, and carried them to that place. They said it was now the third day laying there unconscious.

Their bodies were very weak due to days of not eating; they managed to eat some soup, goat meat and papa. It could be seen from the outside that the weather was clear, but snow was still much on the ground. No one could move from one place to the other. They were just glad that they survived their death. The first thing they did when waking up was to turn on the radio, they were very happy when they hear that the soldiers took over government and they were already preparing for the national election day. They all exchanged hugs, and said "mission accomplished".

TP-"Let nothing like this ever happen again to our beloved nation, but if there happens again to be ruled undemocratically like in this past government; then we would be left with no choice but to start a war again".

They had to lie low for the rest of that month; no cell phones were allowed to be opened, so they had cut ties with the whole outside world. You know life without a cell phone is difficult especially in these days of social media. After a month they opened their phones. The first message they got was that, most of their key informants had been arrested...Jerr! Shit had just hit the fan...

## Summary of chapter 10

In this chapter, TP find himself in prison, not knowing how, but last time he checked they arrived in town and something heavy hit him on the head. The cell he was in is not conducive. The guards came and took him to the magistrate Court and they told him he ran a conspiracy to topple the government which he succeeded so he should wait in a maximum prison for his trial. He receives a letter patched under his food plate, coming from his friends saying they are working on realising him. He find from the newspaper that army boss had been assassinated during the time of topple, he losses hope as his friends do not fulfil their promise. Emm, Justice and guards helps TP to escape prison on 31 December. Amy boss wants to see him immediately. Characters are TP, Emm, Justice (big three) prison guards and the army commander.

## Chapter 10

"I am okay, you`re okay, now let`s go to work"- *Albert Schweitzer*

The room was in complete darkness, only a small hole, yah, a hole, it can`t be said it was a window because of its size, it brought in a reflection of a light in the room. He was in that tiny room with a mattress and a black blanket; no pillow! A small urinatingand defecating tin was put beside the mattress, the room was covered with cement, on walls and on the floor, the door was made of a metal that only had a small opening, though no one had ever opened it. He wrapped himself with that shit smelly blanked. He discovered during minutes of thinking that he was wearing a maroon jersey and an orange trouser, he was in prison.

The last time he checked they had just arrived in town at his place, he remembered opening a door and boom! Something heavy hit him on the forehead and he couldn't remember what happened afterwards. His thinking was interrupted by a noise produced by a door while opening, while waiting to see who was about to enter; within those seconds police constables entered very fast, put a black cover on his head, cuffed his hands and dragged him out.

They were holding him in the armpits dragging him outside; through the holes on the black cover he could see a little that they were heading to already awaiting vehicle which was surrounded by police constables and soldiers. All of them were fully armed, with machine guns and AKs, they shoved him into the vehicle and they hit the road. They only uncovered his face when the vehicle stops. They took about 15 to 20 minutes to reach to that destination; they then shove him out of the vehicle and yah! They were at the magistrate court.

He was put in the box and within minutes; -"Mr TP; you are accused of running a conspiracy to topple the government (which of cause you succeeded), and leading to loss of lives; you are free to find a layer and if you cannot afford it, the state will offer you one, you will therefore remain in a maximum prison while awaiting your trial".

As the magistrate was reading those long sentences, TP was smiling from ear to ear after hearing that the government had actually collapsed.

To achieve something in this world, you should be willing to give out whatever you`ve got to achieve it, even your life if there is need.

They drove him back to the maximum prison like they were instructed, still black cover covered his head, and they shoved him into the cell again. At the time he was wondering where his friends were and he just hoped they were still alive and if they were; it would mean one thing; - that the game is still on and they were just getting started. While still having a chat in his head, a small opening from the door opened and someone threw some informative newspapers, his eyes were glued to the heading that said; "Lieutenant General shot dead" apparently things got worse such that some top officials issued an order to shoot and kill the general; the acting general was still on; the new prime minister was yet to appoint the new general.

Still! He knew that things within the army were never going to the same again. Trust within them was never going to be on line within minutes. On other pages was just repetition of what went on before the government topple and people affected and so on and so forth. He didn't care about that, he was just glad that their mission had succeeded. But the question still remained "how was he going to get out of the mess he was in at the time!?"

He knew he still had alliences everywhere though they couldn't be trusted much anymore because of panic and frustration they went through. His last hope was on his friends. The following day, the small hole at the door opened and an arrogant guard said; "Nka ntja" (take dog), he placed a plate containing a slice of papa and three beans floating in brown water- "nxa" TP thought to himself "this guys must be joking, how is such little food going to keep my stomach busy". Before he could insult him, he closed the opening.

While holding a metallic plate, he felt something paper like at the bottom; he didn't waste time, he took off the paper which was wrapped in an envelope, put the food aside and immediately opened the paper; it read;

*"Life on the outside world isn't easy, we leave underground but we have eyes and ears on top and on the sky. We are back on track, we recruited some new agents and spy so as to free you, but you must be aware that we have been divided into two factions, though on the same mission; our mission is just to work hard and free you while the other faction still care about you but they are more into the army; they don't like the new commander and they are of a believe that he is the one who let to the death of the late commander. But then, hang in there brother, we are very close, very close -*

*Regards*

*Your true friends"*

The letter cleared his mind. That letter made him to lose appetite; he couldn't wait to see his boys. He owned the system, even the prime minister himself knew, though he wouldn't say it to TP's face, but he knew deep down that he was where he was because of him; maybe it was high time to show a token of appreciation and release him.

He had lost sense of time, the newspapers that kept being pushed into his cell were for the past weeks or months; he knew all what they were discussing on newspapers for he was part of the whole thing. You know when news is on fire, every journalist would want to write about it until it becomes monotonous due to being overwritten; so they were becoming useless each day hence he stopped reading them.

Days, weeks and months passed waiting for his trial but somewhere somehow it looked like nothing was going to happen. No one wrote for him in months and he began thinking that everyone had deserted him. But he didn't lose hope, a little fire kept kindling and yah; he knew that one day he would be a free man.

The following day in the evening, though he wasn't sure which month, he was visited by two guards; the first one was tall, very dark in complexion and very muscular like he was playing for some www E champions; the second one was just average i.e. neither tall nor short, he was the one holding a torch while the tall one was holding a hair clipper which was already on. They were to cut his hair, for he looked like a mad man, the hair was itchy and just too much. They cut his hair very fast and a third guard brought him hot water and some towels to bath, he didn't bath in ages, so he was very happy and surprised at the same time of what was happening.

Many thoughts came to his head but the one that couldn't leave his mind was that, he thought he was being prepared for execution; he knew from his readings that, Lesotho still had the death penalty act; though in his time, no one had ever been executed, but that act was alive. He thought "maybe they are setting example with me", the thought made him sweat, coldness on his back rushed, heat also rushed through his body at the same time and he knew he is seeing shit. But then, he contained himself and bathed while they were standing beside him.

After that they gave him new clothes and the tall nigger said; "happy new year boss… oh! I mean man" after saying that TP could hear sounds and see beautiful colours of crickets via a small hole up his cell, and he knew it was without no doubt 12 o`clock the new year, yah! New year in prison; time flies you know! While still gazing up the mini window, other guard`s phone rang and he picked it within a second; TP could hear someone on the other side of the phone saying "we are ready", and immediately they told him to shut his mouth and follow them, they hand cuffed him and he knew he was about to reach his final destination; everyone was asleep, he could see well because this time he wasn't covered with a black thing around his face.

Instead of taking him anywhere within the prison they took him to the exit door that lead to the outside; the guards just saluted at the main exit, they headed with him straight to a 4*4 vehicle that was ready to move by a show of its lights; he could see from a distance that he knew it, and yah, he knew it because it carried them for over two years now while fighting for the country's freedom... he thought 'it should be written "freedom fighters at the back" for it was about to set him free again.

As they approached the vehicle, they removed the hand cuffs on his hands and wished him fair well. TP thanked them and entered the car where he found two of his friends; yah! The big three were back together again. They hit the accelerator and drove away in some outskirts of town to a big tilled building, where they entered, and there was no one, got into other rooms in silence; that was supposed to be a bed room, but with only one bed, well dressed, they removed it, and where it was, on the floor they pulled a handle up and it opened, giving an entrance down stairs; they entered the down room closed the door behind them.

The room was fitted with new computers and big screens and two computer specialists were there working tirelessly. They said they were working day and night to keep everything back to normal and end up helping with TP's release from prison; they briefed him of what they have been up to and what they intended to do next.

A new commander had assisted them to end up freeing him and he knew the commander personally because he was one of his loyal spy recruits. The commander wanted to see him immediately after being released, for there was something very crucial he wanted to discuss with him. TP didn't like the idea of going there, he wanted to lie low for some time but because he insisted he couldn't refuse. He then sent him a message informing him that he would see him the following day before lunch.

The commander said he shouldn't worry much about his men, and TP didn't worry that much because many of them were under his web, but still he had to be extra careful as he was informed while in prison that there were two factions within the army...he took a deep nap and woke up the following day to grab some tea and prepare himself to go and see the commander accompanied by his friend.

## Summary of chapter 11

TP and his friend got set up, as they went to the commander's office like he asked in the previous chapter, he is shot while they enter his office, soldiers come shooting at them when they come out of the office, a Samaritan soldier rescue them and tells them they were set up. Main characters are TP and his friend, Justice and the stranger. The chapter end with the big three deciding to go home and refresh.

## Chapter 11

"In life, shit happens, that's the fact; and the question is, 'if it does happen, are you ready to clean up your mess? Or you would just leave your parcel and go?' Remember- where you left it might be the same place you would need a refuge in future, so it must be reiterated; learn to clean up your mess". – *Thapelo Potsanyane*

Yah, shit had really hit the fan!

They moved slowly from the commander's office, shaking with fear, if loss of thinking happens at the same time to different people, they would have said they had lost their minds, what they saw was something else; they felt like their hair stood at one end. And yes, if hallucinations too could affect many people at the same time, then they would conclude that they were hallucinating. For seconds they looked eye to eye speechless.

For the record, they came to the lieutenant's office that day; they checked in at the entrance and the soldier who was at the reception called the commander's office to ask if they could go up, after the call he directed them to go up wards on the third floor, they said the elevators were not working so they had to use the stairs. They passed through some scans that checked for availability of weapons, before heading to the commander's office. They had none at all since they only use pens and papers and their weapons were only those too materials in their hands.

They knocked once and entered commander's office, - the next thing they heard was a gun shot and immediately their boots were flooding in blood, the commander lying down on the floor, they did not see where the bullet came from, but the window was broken and surely the bullet came from there. They immediately rushed to the door to the outside of the office. Everything happened so fast, down stairs it could be heard; sounds of boots moving upwards, sounds of guns being cocked and they knew that they were the first suspects. So they headed to the scanners, immediately after passing they were welcomed by gun shots that nearly hit them but hit the walls.

A door just besides them opened and someone pulled them into the office and closed the door. He immediately said, "You were set up, they are going to kill you" and then said they should follow him; they ran to the emergency exit and went down stairs outside. It could be seen outside things had changed, vehicles moved up and down, siring, movement of soldiers, everyone was busy and they knew their lives were really in danger.

Sometimes you have to follow, so as to be followed; sometimes you just have to have faith and things would get better, faith is a spiritual eye, it tells that things get better in the end before reaching them. Sometimes you become blind while you are seeing clearly, but because of the situation you are in, you cannot do anything but just follow your heart.

Just following a stranger was something else but then he rescued them, he seemed like he knew what he was doing, they headed to a near-by military house. It seemed like a store room, by the unpainted plank door, with some machines outside. He didn't even enter a key to unlock the door, he just opened it and ordered them to go in fast, he then said "I have no time to explain anything" he showed them a plastic bag saying; "put on some military uniform in there, we have to hit the road before this place turn red", they quickly put on that uniform which was new and they headed to the other room where the military vehicle was packed.

It was a range rover, he took a key on one front wheel and started the engine; he advised them to relax and he drove. The place was getting uglier, they drove passed many soldiers but everyone was minding his own business. They drove to the main gate where soldiers at the gate stopped them saying, they have clear orders not to allow anyone in or out, shit! They felt like being poured with cold water, TP's friend yellow face turned red within seconds when thinking of turning back, the driver pulled out something card like and handed it to the men at the gate.

They immediately stood still and saluted, opened the gate and apologised and wished them a blessed day. They began wondering who this stranger was; it was their first time to see him for he wasn't in their web of specialists the last time they checked. He drove straight to the save house and they knew he must be trusted if he knew that place. TP had spent a lot of time in prison and he even lost track of their key informants, some would just approach him like they have known him for centuries; but even the friend he was with; Emm, seemed surprised of the whole situation.

TP hated much when they said boss to him, because he just thought himself as an idealist, someone who could think outside the box. When they reach the save house, Justice told them they realised late that they were set up, but he immediately informed his secret informant in the army to rescue them. The guy was a special forces, very high rank and he was also the friend and guard of the commander who just got killed; that's explained why soldiers at the gate respected him so much. They thanked him and made proper introductions.

The way to freedom is crooked, the path to liberation is not smooth at all; success has to be worked hard for, it`s not easy to touch the sky if you are not willing to build a tower. These young men`s lives had never been easy at all but through dreaming and implementing those dreams, they achieved the impossible. The forefathers of the Basotho nation fought countless battles to make a strong nation, to create a path for the future they foresaw.

It could be wondered if they imagined the future of this nation as torn as like that time or the past few years. This world is so cruel, and yah; it`s not for the weak, every man for himself. Most people who suffer are not the bad ones but the good, those people who sit back and take care of their families, those who open their bibles each day and head to church, those community leaders at home; yah, those are the ones who suffer the most.

If you could think deeply and critically, this world is where it is because of good people not the bad ones, this world is full of corrupt politicians; rapists etc. because of good people not the perpetrators. While they seat back and pray for them instead of stopping them, they just continue, while they seat and just say "they are so corrupt" they continue with their corruption, they continue with killings, and you the innocent all you do is just keep clapping your hands together with depressed, shamefulness and surprised faces.

At his age the only thing TP longed for was just his freedom and the freedom of the whole nation. Because if they were free, then everything would be in order and at its original place, they were so focussed on issues of the country such that he even forgot his own family. So he thought after all that has happened, he should maybe head home, lay low a little, live like a normal person and stop playing hide and seek, but the thought that they just escaped their own death gave him some goose bumps.

They used to hunt not be hunted, they were about to stop the game but they knew their death was so close, the only best way was to stay on it and figure out the way forward, try to find who was behind the attack, it was going to be another long story to figure out but it had to be done and done very fast. But then they decided to go home and refresh, forget a little about the whole drama and come back with a good and sharp mind again.

You know there is no sweet place like home. They still had to be extra careful since everyone would be alone in his own home without any back up, and all decided to part ways, and take some weeks at home.

## Summary of chapter 12

In this chapter TP is at home trying to cool off, he find trouble following him as people close to him get killed, his grandmother get shot, on the day following her burial someone who worked for grandma get shot and grandma's sisters son get shot minutes later. This people are very close to him so it hurts him so much, he receives a call and the caller claims the doing. The chapter ends with the last victim being taken to hospital where he dies.

## Chapter 12

It is much better to lose your life than having the pain of losing the people that you love the most, the people who were always around you in sickness and in health, the people who have been with you since you were young until you have fully grown. Life! Death has always been there since the creation of the so call earth, but it is still one of the most painful and unacceptable thing that we experience and pass through whether we like it or not.

At first he thought kids were playing with some milk boxes, you know, when we were young, we used to take those boxes lay them on the ground, step our toe on one side where it has been pieced and step hard on it with another toe so that it could create a gun like sound. So hearing that he thought akha! These kids, the sound went boom, boom again and again. They looked at each other with the people he was with at the taxi stop at home.

Upon hearing the sound they headed where it came from and it was at TP's grandma`s home so they ran straight there. The first thing he did was to rush to the kitchen where he found her lying on the floor, with bullet holes on all her body; his older son had run after the killer, returned after few minutes holding a gun saying it belonged to the murderer; he explained that he was in the gardens when he had the sound, he immediately ran to the house and met the man who did not recognise him. So they fought for the gun until the killer fled for his life and left the gun on the ground.

That was one hell of a thing; TP thought he was going to refresh but no; things were taking another direction, while they were stranded trying to think what to do, a call came from TP`s phone, it was a private caller and the caller went like; "I will hit you where you least expected" and he hang up. Yep! Shit had just started to hit the fan. At the time he felt like his heart stops for a second, perspiration on his forehead started going down, his feet tremble, he wondered who might be the caller but he didn't recognise the voice at all.

Things were heading to a different direction; apparently most people who knew of their web, thought his grandmother were the one financing them since she had money. He immediately made a call to his friends and told them what just happened. He could hear panic in their voices, and he could feel that things were about to get worse; the commander! They were about to get killed few days ago and now his grandma! Thoughts overloaded his mind he couldn't think of anything else, but hey! They created lot of enemies for the past years and it was what they anticipated, that they would never live free after what they did.

It was time to try new strategies, try new ways of finding who were the enemies and the ways to eliminate them, but not completely; just get them off the way, for they were not the killers but strategists, but then if people happen to die, the big three shouldn't be blamed, when one gets to heaven or hell.

Life is just a drama, sometimes it becomes too emotional, while sometimes it is kind of fun. But as of that time, the drama was too emotional it was hard to cope, he loved his grandma with all his heart; when his mom had nothing at all, she was there for her, she sometimes helped her with paying some fees for him, so yes, it was so emotional it was hard to hold back tears.

They had to prepare for the funeral; all his friends came to his home to assist with some choirs. He always said; after the darkest nights, the sun always rises; but sometimes the blackest nights are too long, sometimes we do not get to see when it rise at all, because we are denied access to the other day. This time they broke him into pieces , and he didn't find his other pieces at all, it was like they had removed his soul out of his body but he was still breathing. It was like they had removed his heart while he watched or maybe burned him alive.

That Friday they expected grandma home, and as the siring rang closer to the village, men began sharpening knifes to kill a cow that was to be prepared. According to the Basotho culture it had to be killed once the deceased gets home and men would gather around to send it to heaven, then they would take some piece of meat to grill it, they call it "Mokubeloana" (that meat that get roasted and eaten after killing a cow, eaten by men only in Basotho culture), they were busy preparing a cow when women came running, from upper direction of the village, they were unable to talk properly because of their cry, men immediately rushed to the area they came from. They arrived to the place and a man was lying in the pull of his own blood.

He was someone who was taking care of TP's grandma`s family, took care of animals, it couldn't be said he was a shepherd because he was more like a family member to them. Things were getting harder each day, they were getting very close to the big three, so they had to be very careful, and they wondered if it would be a wise idea to be at the funeral that day and the next day or they should just run. It seemed like somehow he was killing the people closer to him and it was tearing his heart knowing that all the things that were happening were because of him.

While still surprised of what just happened, a gun burst about nine times not very far from where they were. They had to run there, darkness had already filled the whole village, but the moon shined beautifully above their heads while stars directed them to where they were going. Damn it, someone was groaning with pain on the ground, they flashed a torch on him and yah, it was the grandma`s sisters son, he was like a brother to him, they shot him with many bullets but he was still trying to move, and police were underway.

They took him immediately to the car, police would take care of the dead, and they rushed him to the hospital where he was immediately transferred to Bloemfontein where he died a few a days after being admitted.

## Summary of Chapter 13

After the arrival of TP in town at his place with his friends, they get a call from that stranger who helped them escape commander's office asking their where about. Their offices are burn to ashes but they manage to escape, through the tunnel, unfortunately the bombers are already waiting for them. The stranger who once helped them is the betrayer who now kidnaps them take them to the mountains but the men they were with in one vehicle helps them escape in the trees. TP and friends loss one another, TP find himself living in the mountains out of no where, living by hunting and gathering food. Main characters are TP and his friends, the betrayer and soldiers helping with the escape. The chapter ends with TP having a dream, and a thinking of fighting back. And it marks the end of part 2.

## Chapter 13

Life in the mountains was beginning to be enjoyable, he lived by hunting, he had three dogs that became his close friends, he wouldn't go to sleep without meat, sometimes they would go hunting themselves and he would just enjoy meat when they return. He would slice some, roast it and throw some to his dogs. Other times he would go up the mountain just below the huge ugly caves to gather some world grapes; they were black and sweet up there.

When he first arrived at the mountains, he struggled much to making some ends meet, but then he had to develop some survival strategies so he lived by hunting and gathering of world plants and animals; yah, at least he was still alive, where he came from, was too hot, fire was beginning to heat him and his friends. Everywhere he went they were there, it was like they were stoking him.

The country has no CCTV cameras on the streets but it was like they were watching his every move. His friends had disappeared just like that, without any trace, but then he knew where they might be, they had since begged him to escape to South Africa, but he couldn't, as he said that he was not a running type, especially running away from problems, he had to wait for them, he said, if he ran, he would just circle around the same country.

But the game was too tough and the fire was too hot, he had to cool off a little. It happens you know that the closest people to us are the ones who back bite us, are the ones who betray us. You remember Judas! What he did to Jesus? That's what happened to the big three, but then it was their own doing, they had let the snake live among them and they gave him access to their holes.

Sure you remember how they escaped from the military barracks, the guy who helped them escape, the one who transported them to their office, the one they thought was trust worthy (well he was trusted at the time/ or maybe he was trying hard to gain their trust) was the one who allowed water to get in through the back door, or maybe it`s proper to say he was the water himself. Within their arrival from the office while from home he called, asking where they were, and because they didn't suspect a thing they told him they were at the office.

Just after a call, a huge blast or a bomb hit the office, luckily they were downstairs, they could feel and smell fire and smoke coming down stairs that things had turn upside down. They had to pack few things and took an escape tunnel; it travelled under few houses, so they would escape without being noticed. When they reach the escape lit, they opened it nicely to avoid unnecessary noise, boom they were welcomed by AK's pointing at them; it was dark as it was around 11pm. The trusted guy who was now an enemy came clapping his hands; "well, well, well guys I must admit you are very smart, but not smarter than me", he said that and slapped them one by one and said; "take them to the van and let us roll", they forcefully shoved them to the van.

There were three vehicles, the traitor was in the first one while they were in the middle one, and they drove for about two hour's non-stop, they passed one forest. They knew the whole country in and out but the place they were travelling on they didn't know, maybe it was because of darkness, they were still travelling within the forest when their vehicle slacked a little, the guys they were with, were about three including the driver, thus making them six in the vehicle, one of them said; "be ready guys" they didn't know what he was talking about, they thought he was saying they should be ready for their death.

TP could see himself leaving the underworld, all his dreams shutter, he could see heavens opening up for him, angels welcoming him, far away in the beautiful white houses, he could see his mom, grandma and all his loved ones who left the underworld. He could see clearly the story of his life rewinding and replaying in his head. And he smiled as he enjoyed the memories of where he came from. Yah, he was a hustler and still a hustler I ever knew and yes the story of hustlers really never dies.

He could see everything clearly now... boom! Boom! Four times, his thinking was interrupted by a sound of a gun that blocked his ears immediately, he thought he was dying, but looking at himself, he was still alive and kicking. The guys in their van were shooting the van behind the one they were in, and they were yelling; "jump and run" they didn't waste any time, they ran for their lives, they jumped three of them, but TP didn't know where he parted ways with his friends, he found himself just running alone in the midst of thousand trees, in darkness he found himself just running not knowing where he was going, but then he thought "life first".

He ran and ran until he couldn't hear sounds of guns anymore, he was jumping from one mountain to another, it was like each time he ran someone was recharging him with some energy booster, he ran until he couldn't feel his feet. He made a stop in one cave, it was then he felt he was extremely tired. He didn't want to sleep, but he found himself in a deep sleep... he dreamed;

"He was in a dark blue suit sitting down under a tree, it was so hot he hat to remove his upper suit, everything was just tranquil, and everything seemed motionless, it was like someone had sucked the air, and he was in the vacuum, beside him was a brown briefcase , so he opened it. There was nothing except a book titled "The Hustler`s Story Never Die". Because he was bored and tired, he decided to read a book;

*"There was no peace at all after World War 1 and 2, democracy was imposed on African countries, because of lack of knowledge and understanding, they took it thinking it might restore order, politicians began fighting for power, in my country the king was stripped off his powers. Politicians ruled the world, xenophobic attacks began emerging, and it was obvious World War 3 was just on its way. Regardless, no one seemed to care anyway, everyone just wanted more and more,*

*the rich began to be richer while the poor were becoming poor day by day.*

*Nothing at all was right, poor service delivery, corruption escalated but no one did anything to set things straight. The world wasn't a save place at all, Africa began to be another continent we were ashamed of, Lesotho wasn't a home we used to enjoy, it wasn't a peaceful country like we knew it.*

*Then a boy was born in this tiny mountainous country. The day he was born, the sky was covered in clouds, the storm came from all sides, lightning played magically above the sky, men gathered around the crawl they wanted to figure out what was happening, but women came out from a nearby house ululating and saying; 'today the warrior is born. The one who will fight for our beloved country, men began singing Mokorotlo (Sesotho songs), some began moving around hitting bushes with their sticks, others murmuring words after words in the local language while moving up and down with happiness. Everyone wondered what the boy would become; some said he was sent to save the country".*

The book was interesting such that, he didn't even see that it was beginning to be late, he put the book in the briefcase and stood up and he moved, he was going to nowhere, because he was just surrounded by the mountains, and he just went and went until it was dark".

Light flashed in his eyes, some tropes of rain fell to his nose, he woke up, it was early in the morning, he was in the cave and he remembered he moved in there last night, his legs were hurting, he had scars in his legs; deep ones, he didn't even know how he got them, but since he ran like a lunatic while running for his life, he got them that day.

He had to get going, so he didn't waste time, he cut a stick from a tree and lifted himself up and moved on. Still, he didn't know where he was, he was just in deep mountains so he just walked until he was tired, hungry and thirsty, far away he could see something like smoke, he moved to the direction, the rain was beginning to pour cats and dogs, he reached the place and found some boys warming themselves inside the cave. He begged them to join them, they welcomed him, he asked what the district and place was called and they said they were in Mokhotlong district somewhere not far from Lets`eng diamond mine.

He spent that whole day with the boys at their cattle post, and he got going early in the morning, he wanted to be very far from trouble. This is where he found himself gathering world plants and hunting for survival, he would return to his small hart after gathering some food and rest a little.

In a hospital doctors would tell you that, the patient is 'critical but stable', it was the same thing with his life; it was tough but enjoyable at the same time. That same night he fell into a deep sleep and a dream came by, this time he was sitting just outside his hurt busking out the sun with his dogs and he was reading the same book "The Hustler`s Story Never Die", it was a very nice dream and he thought that's why his brain kept replaying the same dream;

*"The boy grew faster, unlike his age mates, he was very intelligent than his age, he strolled the country seeking knowledge, you wouldn`t find him with his peers but with the elders feeding him knowledge of a life time. One day some English men and women came to the village, actually they were just tourists, this is where they met this amazing boy, because his name was hard for them to pronounce, they just called him Professor; yah well, he was really a young growing professor, he excelled in everything he did, he challenged teachers, he challenged lectures at the higher learning institutions and he even challenged the policy makers.*

*He lived in his own world, where no one could ever reach, no one understood how his mind worked, so he didn't have many friends, he made a pen and a paper his best friends, he understood the world like no other, his perspective towards the world was out of this world. He lived in his own planet, for the first time the country came to order as professor became a professor not just by name but a real one".*

Dogs bucked outside and they woke him up, it was already in the middle of the day, he had slept for the whole night and some morning hours. Outside dogs were sharing some piece of rabbit they just hunted themselves. The sky was clear than any other days, it looked like a lie that rain was pouring heavily yesterday, everything seemed clear, the country was green, trees were about to fall with fruits, rivers were overflowing, and he marvelled at God`s work.

He knew that everything that`s green symbolises new beginning, to all plants and creatures that were created by the most high. It was time to do a little introspection, start well with the right foot, for the past months were never easy, they were just hell of the months. Yes, he would have to go hunting first, this time he wouldn't hunt rabbits or catch birds, this time he would hunt his enemies down, he would put a pen down, books aside and he would take a gun in his hand, a knife on the other and ride his bike. He is a hustler for he was born in the family of hustlers hence why;

"The Hustler`s Story Never Die"

**END**

## Summary of Part 3 and chapters 14 to 20

This part entails TP going to South Africa to search for his friends, find them as they were about to start a training where they wanted to know how to shoot and use other weapons of war. TP joins them; they did not know that they were trained to be missionaries who were to assassinate the prime minister of Lesotho. They device strategies on how to warn the prime minister and they succeed; they join forces with the guy who once helped them escape the betrayers trap whom they now call Judas. They want to catch Judas unfortunately the person they are using to get to him also betrays them and end up kidnapping TP whom they tortured. TP scares his friends as he doesn't wake after their doctor made numerous CPRs (cardiovascular Pulmonary Resuscitations). They get betrayed by girls at the party and ends with Justice in Psychiatric hospital and Emm in comma.

## Summary of chapter 14

TP, Justice and Emm find themselves in South Africa training to be missionaries who are to assassinate their own prime minister unknowingly. They warn the prime minister through their informants at the Maseru border gate. They escape as they are on their way to kill prime minister; those whom they were with get caught. The Chapter ends with TP talking with the informer about ways of capturing Judas, while Emm and Justice wait for them to finish. Characters are TP, Informer, Emm and Justice.

## PART 3

## Chapter 14

"Let us get something straight here, you and I are not friends, we are just allied by business, so you better tell me who is your boss's name or I walk and I guess it won't be good for business, would it be informer?"

"Where is my money then TP?"

"You see the guys sitting at the table near the door? They have your cash, so you better start or I walk and you won't like it's"

Sitting at the table were Emm and Justice waiting for TP to give them a signal. This was their first mission after their escape; they were starting to hunt after a long time of waiting. After his return from the mountains, TP went searching for his friends in South Africa where he thought they would be; fortunately he found them right on time. They were to start training with someone who said he would train them on how to shoot and use other weapons of war.

So TP became part of it. Somewhere in Rustenburg, they arrived carried at the back of the van by the transporter; the place was completely out of town. "Guys do you really trust this guy?" TP asked pointing at the driver. The driver was a hunk white man; he didn't say much but sounded like a British by his accent when ordering them to get to the vehicle.

"Yah, we trust him, but like you always say; always expect the unexpected". The place was far but since the pick up van arrived early that day to pick them, they arrived on time. There were few houses or hostel like buildings where they would be staying. "This is your new home, it's not too late to quit because you just arrived in hell, come, let me show you your room, and I will be back tomorrow" the British said and left.

Justice-"well, this place really feels like hell guys, I guess we should just leave". At the time the driver had already drove away. TP-"I kind of like it here, if we quit, we would be surrendering our lives to our enemies at home, but if we do it now, then we will die fighting". The room they had been allocated had four stacked beds, a drawer, and a big watch on the wall that produced an irritating noise. There were also few blankets and nothing else except for their small sport bags.

Outside everything was clear and peaceful, birds were singing melodiously in the surrounding trees and a stream of running water could be heard a small distance from the camp. Emm-"its late guys, we should rest, we don't even know what we are going to do or when are we going to start the training tomorrow". "Yah well you are right" TP said.

...

Cold water splashed on their beds, a horrific laughter woke them, "this is not a hotel or hostel fellas, wake up". They woke with wet clothes, the person who poured cold water on to them switched on the light, "follow me; we have a lot of work to do", it was around 3am. They just followed blindly; pass through few blocks to where about seven people were standing motionlessly.

"Join them, fill up the lines". They obeyed the order and the hunk stood in front of them. "You don't have to know my name, I m your trainer for today and once again, welcome to hell, if you follow my instructions, you will survive, I didn't choose you but you chose me because you have a purpose to fulfill, after the time you will spent here, you will be the best missionaries ever". He didn't say much; he beckoned all of them to follow in the jog like manner out of the camp, they ran near the stream, a little up the pace, they ran until they reach the other place like camp.

They were ordered to enter in some room which had all kinds of training materials for fitness, the room was tidy; they began wondering who does the cleaning. They trained the whole day in that room and during lunch time a vehicle would come by and provide food for them, no one talked to them except their trainer not even the people who provided them with food, it was like they were smeared with a super clue on their mouths.

The group compost of three Basotho (the big 3), two Nigerians, one Indian and four South Africans.  "Lord I hate this place" Emm said. "Yah, it really feels like hell"-TP, "help me lift here Justice, this things are so heavy, pens and papers are the best". "TP stop talking and get going, you said you don't want to quit, this day is very long I wonder when are we going to finish this training!"

"After six months maybe", an Indian ventured in, they all looked at him with surprised faces, "what? Six months! Do you even hear yourself?" "yes six months, he continued, 'my brother happened to be trained by the same guy two years back, and he took a complete six months of training without visiting or even calling us at home. We didn't even know where he was at the time; I just knew when he returned and told me not to talk to anyone about it, not even our parents".

TP-"Jer! This feels like a nightmare, but then, nothing we can do, we have to complete this". Emm-"do you know what we are training for because we only wanted to know how to shoot?" Indian (nicknamed Bushi)-"no I don't know but belief me, it's not good at all, that guy standing there (pointing at the trainer who was busy with the call at the time) is not good at all, but then for myself it's just cool, I like the bad! Lift up, up man, Mr. serious is coming".

"This is where you will be shaping these shapeless bodies of yours to good ones". "This guy is so arrogant"- Emm said after the trainer left. "It`s okay, we will be alright". The sun sets and they returned to their camp, it was each day's training which lasted for about three months and yes their bodies had gained some shapes; the second three months were the months of guns and weapons of mass destruction and lessons about the mission.

"So guys, this mission is simple but complicated at the same time and very, very sensitive, I trained you for all these months to shoot to kill, we don't play with bullets, they are so expensive, it's high time to get to the mission itself. I will be leading this operation with my partners in Lesotho with the help of one of the politicians in there; we want to completely eliminate the prime minister of Lesotho. TP, Emm and Justice; "what?", "Is there a problem there?" the trainer asked, "No, no, no problem sir". "Good, off to your rooms".

The distance was very long to their rooms, they wanted to talk about what they just heard; "close the door quickly: So guys, what are we going to do? We have to tip the prime minister, this can't be happening". Emm and Justice held their heads in their hands. "hell we are in hot water, how are we even going to warn the prime minister when that thug took all our phones and tomorrow is the day when things will be going don't".

"We should come up with a plan, I don't know how, but there should be a plan, no one knows our country like we do, this is why they chose us to be in this mission, do we still have our people at the border gates?" Justice-"yah, I guess so, what are you thinking TP?" "I don't know, we might get separated along the way, some will lead the way crossing to Lesotho illegally with the weapons while others would cross the border legally and if it goes like that, anyone of us who would be taking the legal rout should warn our informants at the gate".

TP was saying this, putting some plastics on the floor imitating the way their vehicles are to travel, showing his friends how they might move. Emm-"And how do you propose we do that man? Are we just going to tell them because I don't think we would be alone in the vehicle even if your prophecy is correct?", "You are right Emm, it would be complicated that way, that's why each one of us will have to write on a small paper and insert it in the passport in the page where it is going to stamped or checked, it would therefore avail itself as the border security controller opens it, then they will inform the prime minister. After that we would have to come with a plan to get away from this people otherwise we would be arrested or be killed alongside them".

"That's quite a plan man", Justice tapped TP on the shoulder, "a good plan in deed".

Early the following morning, the pickup vehicles were ready and just as predicted, there were three vehicles. 'Remember the plan guys otherwise we will all be dead in hours to come' TP said. Just as they foresaw, they were instructed to get into different vehicles. TP got to the one that was instructed to cross the Maseru border while Emm and Justice took the ones that would penetrate through the Mokhotlong district. It was good in deed, for everything worked in their favor, but the escape plan was still a barrier.

Driver, "guys, after crossing the bridge we have to drive to that side of Mokhotlong, boss said we should meet them halfway that side, there is someone he has to meet before the mission". "And who is that? Is he a politician or a priest to pray for us before we die?" (They all laughed). "No guys, none of that, he was very formal when talking to him and he addressed him as boss too".

Thoughts began moving around wondering who that might be, but no one came in TP's mind, no enemies at the time he knew that would want the prime minister dead that bad. Even the politician behind the mission was still a mystery, things were beginning to be much complicated, he wanted to escape at some point, but wanted so bad to see the so called 'boss'. He knew the politician wouldn't dare expose himself; he would just connect with his puppets via the phone. But as for the unknown boss, he would surely want things to go as planned, give clear orders and yah he doesn't care that much, he only cares about the accomplishment of his mission. So hot or cold they would be able to see that boss.

They had already passed the border and the tip given off like planned, now heading to the place where they would be meeting the other teams. Through the phone TP heard that the other teams are already driving between the mountains of Mokhotlong down to Maseru, but they would meet somewhere in the Leribe district, this was the agreed spot for their boss and his boss. It was already late when they meet in one deserted place, darkness had started filling the whole country, they wanted so bad to see the guy their boss was about to meet.

And guess who they saw! From a distance, headlights of the vehicles light them (TP whispering to his boys) "is it my eyes or what guys? Are you seeing what I am seeing?"Emm-"yah, Judas himself", Justice-"who's this guy mar! I thought I knew him, but he is beginning to piss me off". TP (laughing) "does this mean we are working for him now? The guy we went this far so that we could take him down, him and his puppets!" With Judas was one man who used to be the big three's key informant.

"This is one big joke, after their meeting we should find a way to disappear, otherwise we would be in trouble with all of them, and surely the prime minister got the message by now". Emm-"now you are talking, after this we should work on our initial plan 'to take down our enemies and the enemies of the country, and these ones are the first (pointing at others in the vehicles) they don't know what awaits them. After the meeting, Judas and his men drove away and TP and others headed to Maseru.

It was around 11pm, and from what they have been instructed, the mission would be carried out the following day since it was too late, meanwhile, they slept in the bushes in the Leribe district. Around 2am, TP- kicking Justice and Emm on the ribs, "guys, let's go" (whispering) "Okay" they tiptoed further and further from the vehicles until they were able to properly run. They at least managed to escape; they moved along with foot, and they took their guns along with them.

When the sun rises, they board a taxi to their new place in Maseru. And they decided to live together this time; this thing of separation they figured would bleed them. The following day, tables had turned, three vehicles and about fifteen men arrested on an attempt to kill the prime minister. By the atmosphere of the city, it could be seen that the country had increased the number of the security personnel, police vehicles and soldiers moved up and down the streets.

A days pass by; "I think we should call that former informant of ours, so that we talk him out to give up his boss (Judas), you still have his number"-TP, "yes, it's still here" "alright Justice, make a call, set us an appointment with him, I pray he doesn't betray us like his boss". "Do you think this is the right idea TP?" "Yes Emm, this is exactly the right one, it is the right time, when they all have scattered, and everyone is at his home now trying to cool off since their mission didn't succeed.

It would take time for them to rejoin again and plan their next step, so it is wise to hit them while they are resting"-"and how are you planning to do that man?"-Justice asked.

"That's a very important question Justice, first we call this guy, set an appointment with him, it seems he is the right hand man of Judas, let us get into his head, into his mind, we want them be divided because you have seen from our last years of work that, we succeed much better when the opposition team is divided.

In that way, they would first fight amongst themselves and then we would come up and finish up where they left. Remember, we should always leave a room of disappointment and a room for another plan. If this plan doesn't succeed, we would have to come back and plan afresh".

The day of their meeting with the informant arrived, the meeting was held in one guest house in Marakabei in the Maseru district, just before reaching Thaba-tseka district. This was to avoid being spotted by people they didn't liken around town and so as to protect their informant and also because the guest house was much comfortable in the outskirts of the villages, up the hills.

"So where is your boss? I asked you this question a million times but you don't seem like you want to give him up. "No man, it's not like that, I just want to know how you guys are going to protect me because that guy is a bad ass, once he spot or hear that I betrayed him, he is going to kill me and my family, you remember what he did to your family, do you want to feel that again?" TP-"shut the fuck up and be a man, you said you want M800,000 cash, those guys I showed you are having it, and with it, you can sent your family away and if you do that, nothing bad will fall onto your family.

I can't guarantee your protection, but you can protect yourself", "how?", informer asked "man, man, man, you have loyal men under you, recruit them just like I did in our old times, I gave you in hand, you were a loyal key informant, you rescued my life countless times, remember that day, Judas and your team captured us, you managed to rescue us. That showed me, you are still loyal to me and I can trust you. Remember how we worked together for the past years, how we toppled the government that was oppressing our people and restored our own government, the government of the people!

Ask yourself man, why your boss wants the prime minister dead so bad like this? Huh?" "He said it's for greater good". "It`s for greater good for whom, for you or for himself? Listen here informer, this guy is working for the opposition party and the only way they are going to back to government is by eliminating the prime minister. Many peoplehave lost interest in them, so they have to eliminate the problem standing between them and the government. Think man, think". At the time TP was tapping his own head with a finger.

For about five minutes the informant kept looking at the ceiling digesting the unknown. TP knew he got into his head. After minutes of silence he said "well, I get your point man, let's do it, just like the old times, keep the money, you might need it to run incase things go wrong". "no man, I am tired of running, this time I rather die, Judas is out of hands and he needs to be brought down as soon as possible".

"Alright Mr. TP, give me a month and I will report progress to you, in the meantime stay low and let me play it my way".

"Let us drink to our new beginning, come on guys (TP calling Justice and Emm) let's have a mini party here and celebrate our new beginning". It was already late and very dangerous to drive to town since they were already drunk, so they booked some rooms and took a nap that night and started their journey to town in the morning.

It is true that, when you are waiting for something important to happen, time seem to be a little slower, some people say it's just the attitude or the mood of the mind. Time is constant but our minds are like controlling it, it goes with our emotions, when we are good, it goes faster but when going through difficult situations, planning something that seem like it wouldn't see the light of the day, it moves like a tortoise.

The big three didn't receive any calls from anyone including their informant in a month. TP-"we should be careful guys' maybe the spear has turned on to us, that guy might have given us up, why hasn't he called us so far?""Yah! We always trust the wrong people"-Emm. Justice-"patience guys, let us have a little faith, he will come around, maybe his plan didn't go as he anticipated". "Yah, let's wait and see".

Before the end of that day they received a call from the informer saying they have been divided into two factions, things became ugly so they are on the run, him and his men. 'Where is Judas? 'Your Judas is still alive, he has a camp in Mokhotlong, if you still remember the road we took that day we abducted you guys! Follow it; it leads straight to the camp though I don't think he is still there, he knows imam working with you again, he won't risk being in that place for long.

'Do I seem like I still remember that road man, it was very dark and we were extremely afraid, I can't  remember but like you said he won't be there anymore. Where do you think he might be if he is not there? Again I think you might consider coming to us, it's too hot for you out there, and they are going to hunt you until they find you.

'No TP, this place is the safest; Judas is a secretive man, I don't know his other places but I once overheard him on the phone that he has another camp in the matter district. Man that guy is very dangerous. Did you even know that, he was the one who set you up when the commander was killed? "No I didn't, so why did he rescue us? Because Justice called him unexpectedly so he didn't refuse to help you because it would blow his cover, he wanted to tear you apart on the inside so he thought it would be right to rescue you so that his mission could still proceed of which it did proceeded and he hit you once, twice and the third time".

'I guess he would be in the camp in Mafeteng to train them and give them a new mission, and if I were you Mr. TP and your team, I would run for my life'. 'I used to run my friend, that time I fought with a pen and a paper, planning strategies to eliminate my problems, so like I told you, I am tired of running, we are ready for anything that comes our way, we have enough weapons to defend ourselves and prepare your men there, I will tell you a day when we pay a special visit to our little

Judas.

It would be ugly and I want to know if you are with us on this one informer'. 'Like old times, I will ride a horse with you wherever you go, and if your horse fall you down then it would be better for mine to do it too. I won't run and if I fall, I will fall besides you my friend'.

## Summary of Chapter 15

In this chapter we see the Informer whom TP trusted flip sides, works with Judas. They found where Judas is so they head to his camp, unfortunately they were running into a trap, but they have a plan they leave Emm and Justice with the vehicle and TP wend where they thought the camp might be with Informer's people. TP get caught in the trees, find himself in a room. Main characters are TP, Emm, Justice and Informer

## Chapter 15

"If the prime minister dies, his blood would be on your hands, no one would be there to protect you, and I wonder where your so called friends would be". Yah, they say when days are dark friends are few. But sometimes they are not there not by choice but because they are forced by circumstances to not be there. "I don't want to kill you TP, like I said, I will fall where you fall but first we should enjoy watching the games we created.

I see you take this things personal, but to me they are just games, and from the beginning you are the only one who gave me some challenge, so yes I wouldn't want to see you die so soon my friend, for we have a very long way to go". The voice sounded familiar but relating the words and the current situation by TP wasn't easy. At the time they had covered his head with a black cover, his hands tied together by a long rope from the roof.

"Where is your two stubborn friends Mr. TP? Where are day?" Honestly he didn't know, for the last time he checked, they had prepared their selves to go to Mafeteng, guns and granites were ready in their car and the informer's team was ready too. They had tipped the police commissioner of what was about to go down, and begged him just to stand by with his men.

They hit the road, it was around 6pm, they wanted to arrive at night when all are asleep so that they catch them without any problems. In the vehicle was TP behind the wheel, Emm, Justice and the informer, the informer's men were tailing them with three vehicles making the number of vehicles to be four in general. This was a very important mission; they knew many wouldn't make it alive because Mafeteng is one of the very dangerous districts within the country.

TP-"People die day by day, men mostly, there are more widows and orphans than any other districts and all who died, died by gunshot; people there fight for blankets differences, some wear yellow Aranda, others black, red or gold and others fall under the main ones which are yellow and black. All this groups has members and their means of survival is famo music. They produce this music in South Africa; insult one another on their records and then end up with killing each other.

So yah, Mafeteng is one hell in Lesotho, and guys if Judas joined forces with those people in Mafeteng then things are going to be very bad, those people are animals, they can kill you and all your family members, and the worse part is their fights has extended to politics. A certain faction goes with a certain politician and the other faction likewise; this is why I am not even surprised that Judas joined those people, his master goes along with them.

By the way, who is Judas's real name? We always said he is Judas because he betrayed us. Informer, sure you know his name, who is he?" Nah! Guys no one knows this guy's real name, we just call him boss, you told me he gave the soldiers at the gate his card that day he rescued you, and didn't you see his name?" "No, we didn't, and we didn't even care at the time, we just prayed we pass those guards safely".

"Yah TP, no one actually knows this guy even where he comes from, he doesn't talk about himself and his family at all. "Alright, let us go and eliminate him, for he doesn't exist already".

The vehicles had already reached Mafeteng, now going into the rural areas of the district to a place called Thabana-morena, the hot spot of the killings of the district and the country in general. "We are very close guys, just turn right and the camp is on the other side, I guess we should leave the vehicles here to avoid waking them up". "You are right informer let's pack here, but I feel some birds in my chest, it's like we are running into the trap; okay guys, Emm and Justice, you wait here with the vehicles, I will give you a signal when I say you come with the vehicles". "Alright TP, be safe". "Sure, be safe too and guys if you don't hear from me in 30minutes you run and go ahead with plan be". (He was whispering to his boys at the time).

Few trees that they entered were scary and out of the trees they couldn't see any camp, when turning back to the informer, whispering; "man where is... (Something very heavy hit him on the forehead) and that was the last time he recalled what happened.

In the room only one person entered once in a while to torture him, then when it's late (it had to be late times as everything become silent) they would pull the rope down and allow him rest on the floor. The place wasn't a prison it was worse than a prison cell. Rats would play on him, but he just let them, his eyes partly closed, ribs hurting and everywhere in his body was blood. He thought death was a better place to be at the time, there was no hope at all. The sad thing was that he didn't even know where he was.

Last time he checked, he was in the Mafeteng district, now knowing not if they transferred him to the other place or district or not.

You know, Barbara Hall once said; "the path to our destination is not always a straight one, we go down the wrong road, we get lost, we turn back. Maybe it doesn't matter which road we embark on. Maybe what matters is that we embark".

He felt like he was just traveling a road that isn't easy to navigate, there wasn't a clear path, or the thing he has been fighting for was invisible, and he felt like he has been fighting for none. Every time he felt like being very close to completing his mission, something else just pop out, out of nowhere, but then it doesn't matter the road but the fact that he embarked on such a road matters the most.

Sometimes when life gets hard, the only thing you can think of is just leave the underworld, for the world of water was better (while we were still in the womb) you know nothing at all at that time, you live in waters that make life much simpler, no problems, no hunger, nothing, you are a hoping to be something one day, of course the hope is not from you but from those expecting you. Then in a certain date after nine months they deliver you in to the world, the world of matter where you strive hard for your life to matter.

This is the cruel world, which is very hard to escape its cruelty, but then, we live in it because we have no choice but the choice is brought by life itself. Then we think sometimes, yes sometimes when things get tough, when things do not go accordingly, we think, maybe that world of spirit is much better. But the thought of leaving this world of matter without putting on a little fight put much pressure and gives headache into a man's skull. That's what kept TP alive, to give it a little fight, maybe the light might appear at the end of the tunnel.

...

Cold water poured on his body; "wake up, wake up, wake up dog, you are not going to die yet, we have a very long way to go". This time he could see a little with one eye which was partly closed due to torture. Two men were standing in front of him, the first one was the traitor, Judas himself and the second one was... what the fuck!!!

## Summary of chapter 16

In the last chapter, we saw that TP got caught in the forest, apparently, Informer and Judas are working together and Informer is Judas's boss. TP is tortured and harassed, fortunately plan B is already in play where by Justice and Emm had escaped and found informer's family, the chapter ends with TP telling Informer that he knows his name which is Phafoli and telling him that his family will get hurt if they kill him. Main characters are TP and Informer (Phafoli).

## Chapter 16

This was the road less travelled, for the vehicle was bumping from one stone to another, from one bush to the next, but they kept moving forward. No one would come to his rescue this time; everything was just out of control. Each day they changed places, the only person who could trace them would be a highly trained person, who has solved numerous crimes, he/she would not be found in the country. This country is too primitive to such an extent that even the recording of day to day activities is still done in books at the police stations.

In this country it is the survival of the fittest i.e. everyone for him/herself, kill or be killed, but then, it would be better to die for a dream than to die dreamless. They say if you are not ready to die for it then you are not ready to go for it. If he dies he would die fighting, he hoped to see himself as a professor one day, standing in front of thousand students at the National University of Lesotho motivating them or just chilling happily at home  with his family.

It seemed nothing was ever going to work, he didn't care much about having a girl friend or live a normal life, he just didn't care at all, all he cared about was the freedom of his people, for if he gives up, it would mean a dictator comes back in to power. It was therefore better to die before that day comes, to leave this cruel world because the world of spirit might be much better for there are no fights over power or money. It's a peaceful place they say.

He rubbed his eyes like he was seeing a ghost; "what!" TP said with a surprised face "hah, hah, hah, yah! It's me my friend, me in flash, you know you have been playing with fire for too long, and I like your game, you are just like a child thinking you can just do anything you want, but that day you tipped the prime minister of my mission was the day you made me hate you. I am going to hunt that prime minister of yours and your two friends and just kill them in front of you, then you will feel the pain I felt when you did that, the amount of money you cost me, which of course you will pay with your life when time goes on".

It hurts so much trusting the wrong people especially in a fight where you might loss your life at any moment. But not this one, TP recruited him, made him somebody in the army, it's true he turned and worked with the traitor but after what they discussed a month or two months ago he didn't think he was playing them. He thought he was one of his team now, he thought he was somebody to be trusted, only to find out that he was Judas too.. no, no, not this one, he doesn't deserve to be called Judas but Legion himself, because he was bigger than Judas and  in fact he is the one who instructed Judas to fall into bad deeds, that's life.

"Yes my friend it's me, informer himself, and hey man, remind me what you and your friends call him (pointing at Judas), hah, hah, hah, they call you Judas, and let me think about what you are going to call me! Eh! Satan! Hah, hah, hah, hah, you would be right if that's my new name, I am the one who brings wrath to Lesotho and I need you to watch every step I take so that you learn".

"You are nothing like me, (TP whispering) you traitors, you are a disgrace to your own country and traitors like you don't live long". "It`s nothing personal my friend, it's just business, business my friend, and you were becoming very bad to our business. The only way to control our business is to control you". "You know what traitor, this is a web, and I don't see by any means you are going to win this war, this is far greater than you, if you were there when I developed this, I said, I want to develop something impenetrable but that which can penetrate into every system.

I am everywhere my friend, I mean everywhere, even among your own people, I am there, in your own family I am there Mr. Phafoli (informer raise his head like he heard the ghost, surprised and angry at the same time). "How do you know my name you mother fucker?" "I know everything about you my friend, remember you were once my pet and all the people that were and still under me, I know everything about them.

I know about your wife who is dying from cancer at the hospital, I know about your kids who are in secondary and high schools, I know your physical address. I know you think you are trying to do the right thing by capturing me, torturing me and doing all this things you are doing, I know you are only trying to make money for your family. I understand because I would do the same thing if I was in your shoes, it shows the human being in you".

"Shut up (he was moving up and down in the room confused) what makes you think I won't kill you right now?" "Because you love your family Mr. Phafoli and you won't want to see them getting hurt because of you; so in that way you won't kill me because that would be your loss and before you go anywhere, I want to tell you something; they are only using you because you are desperate, after completing their tasks they would just chuck you away like a used toilet paper".

Phafoli and Judas went outside, closed the door forcefully and left TP alone. In everything you do, always have a plan B and that plan seemed like working just right. TP (recalling) *"guys I don't feel like I trust this informer of ours, it just feels like he is hiding something big from us. So I want us to dig up everything about this guy, where he lives, his family, how many times they eat, how many times they go to toilet etc. And compile that data in case things don't go according to plan it would work in our best interest". "You are right TP, I don't trust him too; let us work on that this month as he proceed with his plan with Judas".*

Outside the door could be heard Phafoli and Judas`s voices and it didn't sound like they were having a good time. It sounded like they were arguing over a very important issue, the next thing that was heard, was gun blazes, once, twice and it was becoming very serious, the next thing the door opened!

...

Mark Heprin says; "from long familiarity, we know what honor is. It is what enables the individual to do the right in the face of complacency and cowardice. It is what enables the soldier to die alone, the political prisoner to resist, the singer to sing her song, hardly appreciated on a side street".

Never change your goal but a plan, a goal should be static, but plans can be changed from A to Z, as long as they serve one goal or purpose. You see, every night we go to sleep with a dream and plans to achieve the following day, but none of us really knows what tomorrow will bring to us, but its faith and hope that keep us moving forward.

Sometimes we just have to hang in there, sometimes you feel like, your life is at the brink of leaving your body, but that spark within you is what keeps you moving to the Promised Land. The door opened and suddenly about five men entered the room, dragged him out of the room to the vehicle that was ready to go. Outside was blood and fire, couple of men lay down motionlessly, It seemed things got really bad, Phafoli was on the other vehicle that followed the one TP was in, they shot him in the shoulder but at least he survived, that's the cost of betraying someone who trust you.

It`s not always the case that the betrayer gets away with what he did to the betrayed, it's not always the case that the murderer gets away with murder, even after years of silence, one day things just pop up. In one village in the country (Lesotho), there are great murderers in the country, one of them was the one who murdered about three boys; brutally murdered them with a grinder and cut them into pieces, but you know what! There would always be something that leads to something and the murderer got caught.

Even the greatest murderers in one rural village in Lesotho got caught, this guy killed about eight women in cold blood, one of the women was a student, who went missing for about ten years but after those years information kept leaking and he got arrested, and uncovered the dead girl where he buried her. But as we speak, he is out of prison, he just took months and got released, that's the system that governs the people of this beloved country, one gets arrested today and tomorrow they are out. And that is what TP and his friends are fighting for, for justice, good service delivery and most importantly fight the bad guys.

The vehicles took the Maseru direction and it was clear they were returning him to his place. "You are always lucky; I wonder which traditional doctor you are paying or the traditional herb you are using. I think I should join your doctor too"-Phafoli said just when they arrive at TP`s place. Emm and Justice were already waiting. "Brain boy, no muttie, no doctor, just brain, I think you should come to me again, you still have a lot to learn, I think I didn't recruit you well enough".

"By the way, where is your friend, Judas?" "He ran with couple of his followers, I don't know where he might be by now. He is the one who shot me that stupid, I gave him all he has but he chose to shoot me instead. I will hunt him to the end of the world". "But you are the one who betrayed the mission, he is still loyal to your bigger boss and you are not, so imagine who will hunt who, who has more resources? I still maintain you come back to the team, you see now you did exactly what we had initially planned. You implemented that same plan...

Hah, hah, hah, I see you wanted things go your way. By the way, we still have your cash here, take care of your men and your family with it, we have enough here". Justice handed him a briefcase. "Thank us later, I speak this while your men are still listening, come join the team, leave by our rules and let us plan together the way forward". "I will think about it TP, you guys take care".

Sometimes you just have to do good to those who did or do bad to you, even the book of the books says that; if your enemy slap you on one cheek, offer him the other. The motto of the big three says 'Do good all the time', when you are being watched and when you are alone with no one watching you, always do good regardless the situation you are in. "Emm call the doctor now, I really need to see him, you see how I am, it has really been long weeks of my life, long days and weeks of torture; I really need to see him otherwise..." He failed at the spot.

## Summary of chapter 17

TP is in comma, their private doctor is trying to resuscitate him, and hisfriends are emotional and beg the doctor to wake him. This comes after the torture he experienced in the last chapter by Phafoli and Judas, so upon his arrival at his place, he fainted. Hours after he woke they decide to throw some party, a girl (Thandi) come to their apartment and ask to join them with her other two friends. Main characters are, TP, Emm, Justice, Doctor and Thandi.

## Chapter 17

"When you were born, you were crying and everyone around was smiling. Live your life so that when you die, you're the one smiling and everyone around you is crying" and Louis L'Amour says "There will come a time when you believe everything is finished. That will be the beginning".

He felt life has escaped him, as he could see men in white and the other one in torn clothes. The one in torn clothes was insisting TP worked for him, but the one in white said "he worked hard for the freedom of my people against you there for he worked for me, go to your place". TP wanted to ask where he was but words failed to come out of his mouth. In the room the doctor was moving around "hold here Emm, don't just stand there like a pole, help me guys, I am going to do the last CPR (cardiovascular Pulmonary Resuscitation) and if he doesn't wake up, we would have no choice but to take him to the hospital, otherwise we will lose him".

"Do whatever in your power doc to save him; what are we paying you for" said Justice with a very cold voice. "'Okay, okay, I will do what I can". He went on with CPR and TP ended gaining his consciousness. His friends thanked God and doctor for saving their friend. "What guys! It's like you have seen the ghost, what's the matter with you?" "Fuck man, you nearly kicked the bucket". Their eyes were brimming with tears, unknowingly, whether they were tears of joy that their friend is alive, that they saw the Greatness of God or maybe because they thought they lost their friend.

You know, life without friends is such an empty one, those people who have been beside you for your whole life, in times of happiness and in times of trouble; TP thought of how much he loved his friends, they have been together like forever, and they used to party a lot. You know Justice doesn't drink alcohol at all; TP and Emm drink a lot but can spend months and months without alcoholic drinks.

When they do have a party, Justice would be the one drunk like no other, drunk with happiness, with juice  that he would keep drinking the whole night of the party. After all the drama, they decided to throw a little party the three of them. They wanted to invite their female friends but unfortunately they didn't think of any, their work had put them in isolation so much that they lost contact with everyone, they had no girlfriends, for they were too busy for such.

They didn't have a reliable space, they moved from one place to another and from what they went through in the previous months, they couldn't risk going home to their families. "How about you call that ex of yours TP? Maybe she could invite couple of friend" "No, you are mad Emm; don't want to meet that girl". This is the girl who nearly killed him with heart attack. He loved her with all his heart but as time went on he found out that she was cheating him.

You know heart break can kill you, and of course many have died because of heart breaks, some committed suicide while others got mad, others killed those people they thought they loved so much, hence TP wouldn't risk calling that girl. While they were still wondering what to do, someone knocked at the door and they wondered who that might be; a female voice "it's me, Thandi, a neighbor here" Neighbor! No one ever came to their crib before, but then since they have been moving from one place to another, they didn't know much about people living around there.

"Okay, I am coming" Emm invited her in, it was already evening and they had nothing to eat, they had been thinking much about the party without even realizing time had gone. The girl was beautiful like an angel, nice body, everything was just in place, God was probably in a good mood when creating that one, it probably took time for her to be manufactured. The big three's eyes were glued at her like they were seeing something from the other world.

Justice's hand partly covered his mouth while widely opened. Emm opened his big eyes widely like he was already undressing her and doing the do's, TP's throat moved up and down swallowing saliva. "Guys! (Thandi yelling at them) I have been standing here for about five minutes and all you do is just look at me like you are seeing something that does not exist!

"Ah! Eh! Okay! How may I help you? Anything for you", Justice said that before anyone could figure out what to say. "Okay, I and my friends want to go out or throw some party, do you mind joining us?" Before anyone could answer again, Justice replied; "no love, no problem, actually we were about to go buy some drinks". "Is your friend okay? (Pointing at TP) I don't think he will be alright having booze in his condition". "No, don't worry about him, he would be alright", "alright I will be back in few minutes, I am going to inform my friends how things are to be", she moved towards the door with a huge smile on her face.

"Hey pretty, don't you need a company, it's not safe outside" Justice said. "No I will be fine, but thanks hey". Emm couldn't stop himself from laughing at Justice as the girl shut the door. "What man! You don't even know the girl but you are agreeing to everything she is saying, have you lost your mind?" "Maybe I have lost my mind man;I have never seen such a beauty". That's Justice for you; maybe people who say men who doesn't smoke or drink alcohol are the most cheating men on earth are right, while you are busy with booze they are busy flirting with girls, and today Justice proved exactly that.

The girl had returned with her too friends, very beautiful but not like her, they all decided to go in town before it was too late to buy some booze , but TP decided to stay home and rest a little before they could party. "Guys don't forget food, I am dying with huger". They parted and TP took a nap.

It is better not take life personal, take it as it is, though sometimes it becomes personal to us, but just take it easy. They say let the past go and live today so that your tomorrow be the best one, but sometimes our past is what keep us on track, for it is by knowing and keep recalling where we come from that we have a clear picture of where we are going, what is expected from us and what we expect to achieve. Sometimes when thinking hard about life, you will see that, the world is torn into pieces like this because we lost your path, we lost our culture, hence why it is said that the nation without culture perish.

Sometimes you just have to forget everything, lead your mind to the world of empty, live your today like it's your last, and enjoy yourself to the fullest, such that if you part ways with the underworld that same day, you die with a huge smile on your face. The night was young and everything was just going fine until...

## Summary of chapter 18

The girl (Thandi) who came to the big three's house in the last chapter betrayed them; this chapter describes how the party went and how it ended. Their house is burned to ashes, Emm is in comma, and Justice got missing. TP join forces with Phafoli at the end of the chapter. Main characters are TP, Justice, Emm, Thandi and friends and Phafoli.

## Chapter 18

Sometimes it's so unfair you know, life isn't fair at all, no it isn't. Tic, tic, tic sound made him nauseous, while tears filled his eyes, a huge lump blocked his throat, the pain was just unbearable, no one seemed to care at all, everyone just performed his work duties like there was nothing, out the window cars moved up and down the street, street vendors selling their fruits and other things.

A cue going to the doctor's office was long and some pastor was giving out the word of God to patients and he read from his Bible Ephesians chapter 2 verses 1 – 5, "and you he made alive, who were dead in trespasses and sins, in which you once walked according to the course of this world, according to the prince of the power of the air, the spirit who now works in the sons of disobedience. Among whom also we all once conducted ourselves in the lusts of our flesh, fulfilling the desires of the flesh and of the mind, and we're by nature children of the wrath, just as the others.

But God, who is rich in mercy, because of his great love with which he loved us. Even when we were dead in trespasses, made us alive together with Christ (by grace you have been saved)".
As he read, TP was praying for his friend to recover, you know when things are not going well in our lives, it's then we remember that God still exist, we forget him when life is beautiful and everything is beautiful.

If God was on earth, people would go on strike each now and then demanding Him to work according to their wishes. It's good that He is not here but omnipresent. Sometimes when you are happy you turn to forget of the problems you are facing, you just want to be in your own world where no one could ever thought you could be. You don't want any interruptions; all you want is just to be happy.

They had arrived with booze and food, and TP started first by enjoying his meal. Boys and girls had already started having their drinks, it seemed they opened them once they got out of the bar because they were each getting to the next bottle, Justice was drinking slowly his Juice sitting next to the window and next to her was Thandi and Emm and the other girl were sitting on one other chair with the girl on his lap. It seemed the drinks were starting to do their work because they were starting to smooch each other.

The other girl was kind of shy, TP liked her, and he thought she was her type since she wasn't a talkative type like him. "Come sit next to me, but hey be careful not to fall on me, my whole body is still painful". "Hey I am not drunk to that extent" the girl replied "what happened to you?" "Car accident" TP lied without making her suspicious. He wouldn't reveal what happened to him to the stranger, he had finished his meal and had started having his hunters gold.

He preferred ciders because he thought they were cool, they didn't give him headache in the morning and apparently, he hated the tendencies of the local peers who would want to drink with you and always want others to buy them some bear; with ciders you will drink until you get drunk, except for ladies who would be dancing beside your table like they know you while they don't, they just want you to buy two or three savannas.

At the moment Justice and the beautiful lady had disappeared but believe it or not, no one saw them when they leave, they were not in two bed rooms nor in the bathroom, they had disappeared unnoticed while TP and Emm with their cheeks were too cozy, they wouldn't spot a thing. Sometimes when you are drunk,alcohol runs straight under the belt and you know exactly what to do especially when you are with someone of the opposite sex.

TP stood up heading to the bedroom and beckoned to his girl, that sitting room wasn't safe; Justice and his girl might pop in any moment. After closing the bedroom door; "where is the bathroom?" TP's girl asked. "Just go through the passage, on your left, that's the bathroom". "Okay, I am coming, be ready when I come back; I want to be your doctor this night". Would you wait? Or you would start removing your clothes fast?, the fact is, you wouldn't wit if you are a man.  About ten minutes passed by, without the girl coming.

TP decided to dress up and go check the bathroom, but she wasn't there, he went to the sitting room, but she wasn't there either. He went to the sitting room to check if she is with Emm and his girl. "Where is your girl man? You look like you have just seen the ghost!" Emm asked, and without answering him, "Emm where is your girl? I thought I would find mine here". Hah, hah, hah, Emm laughed lightly, while smiling from ear to ear with his eyes partly closed, with a drunken voice he said "she went to the bathroom man"

"What the fuck!" (TP whispering) "Man she is not there; I am from the bathroom", "no TP you are joking. I know she is in there". "No man she isn't". TP wasn't that drunk, but Emm was so full, and sometimes you know arguing with a drunken person is just a waste of time, instead of answering your question, they would be talking about something you didn't even ask, or that which you don't even understand. So TP decided to leave him alone and go check the kitchen.

There was no one in the kitchen too, the door was still locked, and they had locked it after realizing that Justice and his girl were gone. TP began to think he was hallucinating, sometimes alcohol can turn you to a lunatic, but to himself he said, "I know I am thinking straight, yah, I am thinking straight" when saying that, he was slapping his cheeks to feel if he could feel himself, he had a believe that when you are drunk and want to feel if you are really drunk, rub your hands on your skin and feel if you could still feel it the way you would feel it when you are not drunk.

Or just slap your cheeks twice or three times, if you don't really feel a thing, know that you are really drunk. He decided to leave the kitchen to go back to the bathroom. In the sitting room, Emm had passed out, with his mouth wide open and snoring like a tractor. In the bathroom there was still no one but something captured TP's eyes, the bathroom window had not been closed, he knew they never open that window at all. And since it wasn't broken it was obvious that it was opened from the inside.

"Shit! Betrayed again!? TP ran to wake his friend, and before he could reach to him... the building was on fire, bricks fell like rain, his head was hurt but he could still think clearly and the first thing he did was to uncover Emm under the stones and the roofing that had fallen down. He found him unconscious, blood all over him but he could still feel his pulse, "call the ambulance please, please call on the ambulance" TP said with tears on his face. He said this to the people who stood by without helping; some were busy taking pictures and videos at that time of the night.

This world is so cruel; how come you don't help someone you see is in pain? Instead you just stand by and take pictures and upload them on social media, that's what people do, they help you when they are done with doing what they are doing on their phones. They are like police who only come to your rescue only when you are done, for instance when you were fighting. At least in some other countries they come on time after being called.

Lesotho police are not like that, they will tell you they don't have a vehicle to attend you, they won't come if you call them saying people are fighting, they will only come when someone is dead to collect him, yah there they will come with pleasure. The ambulance arrived; he was rushed to the hospital.

It was now the seventh day "how is he doctor?" "he is still critical but stable Mr. TP, we are hoping he will get better soon, let us let everything in God's hands sir for now". "Okay doc, thank you, will be in touch tomorrow". "Bye Mr. TP".

...

"You are quite a survive Mr. TP, but next time you won't get that lucky". A text clicked in TP's phone eight days after they have been attacked, the number wasn't working though, because TP had called it multiple times but it didn't exist. Right after the attack he had called Phafoli telling him what just happened.

"Did you sell me out boy?" "No Man, how could I do that" Phafoli with a trembling voice, "five of my men have been killed in the last two days, and I am on run. What's going on man?". "It's Judas; he said it's only the beginning" Phafoli said. "Alright I will make a plan, keep your phone on stupid, I will be in touch".

Justice was still nowhere to be found, TP had pulled all his resources in finding him but all in veil, he just disappeared without a trail like that day he disappeared in the room, but now he disappeared from everyone, days and weeks passed by, no trace of him. Days and weeks passed by with Emm still in coma; there was no hope in everything TP was doing. He was a hustler, but there seemed to be no light at all at the end of the tunnel.

Someone stood at the end of that tunnel therefore making it hard for the light to penetrate through, the way to freeing the nation seemed to be too narrow, the way to physical and emotional freedom seemed to be a long and a crooked path. The way the hustlers travel on seemed to be not just a straight line. When you think you have reached your destination, only to find that you are only at the beginning.

As a hustler, your duty is to work on problems, reduce or eliminate them. The big three tried their best to reduce or minimize their obstacles and to some extent they managed to do so. Now there was only one problem, the problem that needed to be dealt with, with immediate effect, terminate it completely or put it where it cannot see the light of the day, where the light penetrate through a small opening, where you sleep with a blanket smelling shit, with mattress like a slice of bread.

But then giving up wasn't TP's hobby...

Early the following morning, "Phafoli, I need you at my office as soon as yesterday, hurry". "Alright TP I will be there in few seconds".

If you believe in yourself, then you will never quit in whatever you do plus quitting is for cowards. "The web is torn, and the only way to achieve the coming mission is to resuscitate it, to pull everyone together and get everyone into his place, call them, go to their places, use the few men we have to reach our trusted informants and any other important persons to our mission, so let us give it our best, if we die, let us not die alone but with Judas and his master, go tell everyone what I have said and tomorrow let us begin".

Phafoli listen attentively without interrupting, after TP's speech he didn't even say good bye; he just turned and hit the road. If you are willing to give up your life to safe lives then you are ready for your dream. In this world, every man for himself, everyone fight for his or her goal but sometimes it feels good to fight for others, it feels very good to sacrifice for greater things like fighting for your own nation. Not because you want to be recognized, categorized under national heroes or because you want to be famous.

But because of the big heart you have for others, a good and a carrying heart for your own people, and then if you possess that, you are a great hustler and the stories of great hustlers never die.

## Summary of Chapter 19

TP and Phafoli joined forces and went on hunting Judas, they find where Judas camp is, in the Quthing district, TP lead the teams by going there first, do some job, killing job and when the game got tough he calls for reinforcement. Many people get killed. Main characters are TP and Phafoli.

### Chapter 19

So many lives were lost; everywhere you go men were lying down in the pool of blood. He had been captured, with blood all over his face and chest that never stopped bleeding. The medics were already attending him and shoved him in the back of a police car. In the other room that was locked, something was moving and it sounded like it was trying to hit the door. TP slowly went towards the door; "is there anybody in there?" It didn't respond but kept throwing itself to the door.

"I need a hand here" one police officer came; they turned a big lock that looked like it wasn't opened frequently. Damn it, man!

It didn't take timenor energy to resuscitate the web, within days, it was back on track, with both human resources and financial resources, everyone had been waiting for so long for it to get back to work, they were tired of the killings that took place each now and then within the country. People were killed with guns or burned alive and no one took initiative because the group that was doing all this things had many resources since they were financed by a rich politician.

"Have you found where Judas's camp is?" "Yes Mr. TP, they have relocated to Quthing district in the areas of Qhoali, one rural area of that district". "Alright thank you". TP was talking with one of his IT specialists, a man who has been in the web since the beginning; he was one of the people who sacrificed their time and energy to make sure that bad boys go behind the bars.

Everyone worked day and night to find this location, number of men guarding the camp and where Judas would be at the time of the attack, for he was the main target.

The day came as expected, summer rains fell from the sky that night until the morning, a good rain, with no thunder, and it was going to be a very long, long walk to freedom. It seemed like it was going to rain the whole of that day, TP had finished everything, so he kneel down and prayed; "Father, you who have been with me from the beginning up to this day, be with me to complete this final mission, give me power and a sharp mind to achieve today's goal, but if I happen to fall father today, may I please be on the right hand side of your son Jesus Christ, help me God, Amen".

He said the prayer and threw his bag on his back, it was heavy, full of multiple guns and other weapons, he rushed to the garage, he didn't want to use a car that day so he got to his motor bike, started the engine and got on to his way to Quthing. Everything was in order, trusted soldiers and police officials had been informed of what was going to go down that night, so they were just waiting for calls that tell them to go on with plan B of the mission, which was to do the arrests and assist TP in case things get out of hands.

The road to Quthing wasn't that long, as the bike moved like a snake on the grass; it was like it was built on that road for that road. One thing good about the road that pass through to Quthing is that the road is just flat, no stipe places, Quthing is one of far district within the country, one would have to pass through two districts before reaching it. If you are coming from the capital city of Maseru, you would go through the Mafeteng and Mohale'shoek districts and then get to Quthing.

As the sun sets, TP was already assessing Quthing town, ventured in one restaurant to have a cup of coffee, the rain was still pouring, and couple of people could be seen outside with umbrellas and rain coats. The area felt much colder than other district he had been to, except Mokhotlong, Mokhotlong is freezing than any other districts. The area began covered with darkness, so TP knew it was time to get going, to get to the deepest rural areas of Quthing, where according to his findings, there was no electricity, "I wonder what they are using at that camp", TP asked himself, "generator, yah, generator, it has to be".

He had this conversation in his mind as he hit the road to Qhoali, out of the tarred road to the gravel road then to a very big stony road, where only 4×4 vehicles could travel, and it would fit in that road alone, other vehicles coming from the opposite direction would have to wait for the other because they wouldn't be able to pass one another. Very far in trees could be spotted some bright lights and according to his map, it was supposed to be the camp.

In the first villages, lit could be seen, as villagers prepare their super, warm themselves and others just lit that fire to prepare their beddings for themselves and their kids. As the bike passes by dogs bucked ferociously, people stood by the road, this might be because, it was very rare for vehicles to pass through those villages, let alone the motor bikes. There was only one 4×4 van within the one village belonging to an Indian who had a supermarket in the community.

It was used to carry stock, to help the sick for some Maloti and also carry the dead for money, it was a multipurpose van, the problem came when it was broken as it was its habit to do so due to bad road, so it became less and less fit for the road. At the time when it is broken, the sick and the dead would be carried with hands or put on a horse back up the mountain to the main road. Motor bikes passed seasonal, during the roof of Africa games, the whites like to play in the mountains, and so they go there to have fun with their bikes.

He passed those villages and before crossing the river which separates the Qhoali villages and the camp, he stopped, hides his bike, put his bag down and took out two 9mm guns and inserted silencers. It was time to let the games begin, kill or be killed, no more turning back; he crossed the river then to the forest. One by one they started falling down, when things got ugly, he pressed a red button for his team and the security forces which were already standing by. Dead bodies were countless.

## Summary of chapter 20

Justice get found in  Judas's camp, he lost his mind, Judas get arrested and even the politician behind Judas funding get caught but TP is still suspicious that there is one funder for the whole thing, the big funder. Main characters are, TP, Justice and Judas

## Chapter 20

Damn! His lips were dry, with weeks of having less water and food. "Justice?" TP yakked, he looked at everyone, and wanted to run, but they held both of his hands and set him down. "Who are you?" one medic asked Justice, he looked at him "I, I, I, I don't know", "Where do you live?" Nothing made sense to him; for he wasn't himself at all, he didn't even recognize his own friend TP.

They took him to the ambulance and started hitting the road to Maseru.

In this world never trust anyone, yah, you can trust them but never give your all, everyone have a snake part in them, a betraying part, even girls are used badly in bigger games by boys, you would think this things only happen in the movies but they also happen in the real world.

The big three were betrayed by girls, which ended up with Emm in coma in the hospital and Justice too in the psychiatric hospital. Judas was imprisoned and the rich politician got caught too. "But is it over?" the road to freedom is just endless, it needs the heart, courage and a nerve to never stop, never give up.

Behind every rich politician in Africa, there is always a rich white man pushing his own agenda. "Who then is the real funder, if he refuse to give him up like I suspect he is going to do, then this is only the beginning, the big storm is yet to come, so be prepared, you are hustlers, hustle for good, hustle for your children's freedom, for your story will never die because the  hustlers story Never die".

**END**

## Summary of Part 4, chapters 21

Part four is whereby TP returned to school to do his Masters degree in criminology, and after completing varsity he works with the National Secure Services (NSS) for two years and quit his job to for officially open his investigations office. Along his work with his team, they find that there are people looting the resources of the country, and as they are trying investigating the case.

Phafoli got married and unfortunately married to Thandi (the girl who kidnapped Justice), and they discovered that the person looting the resources of the country especially in the mining industry is the boss of Thandi, who is the boss of Judas, who was the boss of the politician that funded Judas. So the game changed they had to hunt down Thandi but Phafoli stood in the way as he protected his wife but he then gave in. Emm dies in hospital after spending ten yes in comma and Thandi claims she is responsible, she kills Phafoli, and kill herself, her employer the looter of diamonds in the country get caught.

## Summary of chapter 21

TP return to school, works for NSS after, but quits his job andforms his own agency, hunting down John (who is also the funder behind the Politian and Judas who were arrested in the previous part and chapters) who works with the minister of mining to steal the diamonds of the country. TP IT specialists get kidnapped, cripple his investigations but they do not give up. Emm dies and someone call claiming responsible.

## Part 4

## Chapter 21

Rivers of tears never stopped flowing, at a certain moment a suicidal thought crossed his mind, but looking back at his family, his young growing children gave him a sense and a purpose to live. If we cud see into the future, see what it holds for us, we would do most of the things we want in life because we would be knowing that at a certain moment in our lives death awaits us. We would just wait for that day to come and then part ways with the underworld.

Death by itself isn't painful, it's just something that clears the way for the new generation, what's painful is the distance we feel between us and the deceased. Memories of happier times we had with the dead are what keep us holding on to them even when they are not there. If we knew what would come our way, we would be prepared for it, if it's a bullet, we would wear a bullet proof, or a car accident, we would just stay at home in doors.

But death is one inevitable bustard that we all have to cross, we may be different in many ways, our skin color, level of life we live in and the countries we come from as well as the continents, but one thing we are all sure is that we share one path and that is death, it is through it that we come to be one thing which is soil.  If we were able to feel whether it's painful or just good when the soul leaves the body, and if we knew exactly where the soul depart to as we die, maybe we would change our perception towards death and maybe we would be so in hurry to cross that bridge.

To us who are left in this world, we feel like we are dying inside when taking a look at the journey we underwent with the deceased, the difficult times we went through together and happy times as they pass through our minds, then with tears and smiles we say, yah! This man lived.

As the coffin taken down to the underground, knowing that, that day was the last time he saw his remains on earth made him to just let tears roll down his cheeks, as the pain slit his heart like a sharp spear going through him and tearing his heart into pieces. They never thought after these many years their friend spend in hospital, in coma, this would be the results.

TP would go to the hospital each day, take few hours, try to give him some food and read him some books, but nothing changed. A complete ten years living a life in trips isn't life, and after what just happened he said, "Maybe it's just okay, maybe he would finally rest in peace,and thisreally wasn't life".

Justice was released from psychiatric hospital after a year and six months, after that, there were no frequent meetings with him and TP, only phone calls. TP decided to further his studies to do the Masters degree in criminology. Life was simple, out of drama, everything was just peaceful, they gave away their office and sold some office equipment, that was what peaceful meant.

The prime minister had changed, he had worn elections like always but decided to retire and leave his successor in the same parry to take over the prime minister's position. The new one was young and energetic, with a smart mind and progress could be seen in development of the country, electricity was installed in the very rural areas of the country, water taps for many people were also installed and the fees in high schools and high level institutions were cut off, hence many things were affordable.

Though some people still didn't like him, but many people believed in him. You know, no matter how good you might be trying to be, people will always find a way to hate you. Someone once said, 'look at the colour of flowers, some have bright colours: white, yellow etc. Red and others, everyone has his or her preferences when it comes to colours, so like it or not, you won't be able to satisfy all the people because they have different preferences, but the majority you touch make sure you touch well so that even those opposing you would see the importance of having you in their lives'.

In school, TP was always on Point and on fire with research in his criminology course. It is true that what we went through determine our way to the destiny we are heading. He didn't think one day he would be interested in such courses but because of what he went through in the past few years, he thought it would be wise to go deep in what in what he had already started.

After completing varsity, one security force within the country wanted him high and low to join them but he wasn't interested in the National Security Service (NSS)though, so after 2 years having been in the job, he decided to quit and officially opened his private investigation Agency.

"When I was young I used to fear monsters, I would hide under my bed when I hear the sound that sounded scary. I was very scared of lightning too; I would hide under my blankets to avoid looking at it. But over the years I learned that everything is a monster if you want it to be, everything is a lightning if you want it to be, what I didn't realize at the time is that the lightning lit everywhere, it just depend on your attitude towards it.

Over the years I realized that, the only way to defeat a monster that made me hide under my bed, is just to face it, and over the passed years I slept in scariest caves, fighting monsters, I decided to face them myself, so being scared is okay, but go out there and face your monsters". That was each day speech TP made to his team, which was hired mostly as personal security personnel for ministers and other people holding lucrative statuses within the country.

So he had access to everyone in the country that could be a potential threat. Like he always believed; where there is money there is always a source so your duty is to find the source and if it's clean then it's alright, but if not, then that is a huge problem. It's true that many people work hard and sweat for their pockets to be full of cash but others take from where they didn't put, while others are given money in return for something, like offering a higher position in a certain government ministry or organization to the payee.

But those are just small things which are spotted in many countries that are developing a sense of corruption in its people. And for TPs business they paid less, so he didn't like such jobs. In one area in Maseru there was a security guard who used to guard a chines company, the guy organized with his friends to rob a Chines man some cash and they did a successful job and got away with one million.

TP's company was given the job to investigate the crime and within no time the guard and the friends were arrested because Basotho have one weakness, when they have money, it speaks louder than they could possibly see. Tracing the guard's bank account was simple, and it spoke languages, that was suspicious as he wasn't earning that much, few months after the incident he quit his job, he threw a party each now and then, only did he not know he was been investigated and he was later arrested.

But cases like these one were simple and TP wasn't interested in them, it's true they brought quick cash in the company but they were small boy's game that is why he always handed them to his subordinates to handle them. Every evening after work he would go home after rough work, play with his kids and spend the evening with his wife. During his wedding, Justice was his best man, he later married and TP was his best man too.

They would go to the hospital to see Emm, with photos to show him, each birthday they would celebrate with him, so that was their daily and yearly routine. The company was one thing that kept TP busy, forgot about so many problems but enjoyed chasing criminals. He didn't stop going to prison to visit Judas; "who is the man funding your master man, you know I can't get hold of your master because of orders from his layers, so I guess you and I can work something out". "No man I am not a snitch, plus, I really don't know what you are talking about, that guy you arrested is very rich he has no funder and I promise you my friend, soon we will be out, you will regret this".

Judas was humble; you know difficult times call for desperate measures. He was right where TP wanted him. The politician's layers had given clear orders that, no one was supposed to see him without them or their concerned, and so it was very hard to get closer to him. Even if he were able to get to him, he wouldn't say a thing, so the only way to be alert of what would happen anytime because of the unknown funder, was to find as much information as he could so that he would be on track with everything.

Maybe it would be wise if he had left everything as it was because you know, sometimes it's just wise to just stick on miner problems because what's hidden below the miner things might be more dangerous than anything you had gone through. But then what's the use of living at all if we can't hunt problems that might be a threat to our children and other coming generations.

"Something interesting came up this morning, one of our colleagues working in one diamond mining company in the country has made a major discovery, for the past three months there has been a private helicopter that landed to the facility, and it lands for few minutes and goes away. In each month, the minister of mining was spotted at the facility the day that the helicopter came, for now we are not really sure what's going on but guys I have a feeling that this one is one of our biggest cases ever, so let us put every resource we have into this case, let go anything and everything you have been doing and focus on this one".

The meeting was held at TP's private investigation office early in the morning that day, it was time to play big boys games, within two weeks other mines underwent some investigations. The mining sales and diamonds that the mines extract each month, the reports made at the end of the year and dividends they gave to the government were gathered. It was discovered that some diamonds were not recorded at all, TP's company had inside men in the mines, who work as just labour's while others held very important positions within those mines.

Something was going on,though not sure what was really going on but there was something. The resources of the country were being looted, and he wouldn't just wait and watched, he knew this was the most dangerous tasks but he went on with the investigations anyway. He took dangerous risks than the ones in the past years. The difference now is that he has a wife and kids, and that, that gave him some headache, so many people he loved passed away years back because of him, so it was hard to put his family at risk of going through what others in his life time went through.

But on the other hand his main priority was also his country, his nation and his people, for he just couldn't wait and watch, there might not be anyone at all who could do the job he does, as the damage or risk would be too much. "Where are about hundred diamondsthese four companies extracted last year, where did they go? It seems they just disappeared without a trace, for sure they have been extracted, according to the pictures and records we received from our people, but they were not published in their reports, where is the money received from those diamonds?

"I assure you my friend's something fishy smells here". "Eh! Sir, you might want to take a look at this, for the past four months before we could suspect the first mining company, the same helicopter had been flying to the three other mines in different districts monthly and what's interesting is that, the minister of mining was always there during those nights, this is according to the CCTV footage we extracted from the mines, what also put a huge question mark is that the helicopter comes with the pilot only, no one else, he would go to the office where the minister already awaits him and then fly off".

"Hm! Good discovery, the pilot to me seem like he is the messenger, then who is the real leader? I guess this is a big question you might be asking yourself right?", "yes sir". "We don't know yet , but very soon we will find out, you know we catch the bird flying each day in the thin air, but we develop strategies of catching it, so it's too easy to catch the one we move around with down on the ground, we will find him or her".

Mining sector has been one of the corrupt sectors within the country for long years, where the government only owns 20% shares and the mining company goes away with 80%, it was one of the sectors that ministers could even kill one another for, so that they could be able to run it. All they are looking for is just to consume and forget about the people who elected them to the positions they are at the time.

That year about five government officials from the mining ministry got arrested in South Africa with the possession of about six diamonds that worth about seven million, they were caught without a trading licence and stupidly driving the mining ministry's vehicle. So it wouldn't be hard to catch those looting the resources of the country, hot or cold they had to be brought down to justice.

Talking about justice, TP had called Justice to come back to the team over months but he just kept promising that he would come, but without fulfilling that. But then he wouldn't blame him, he went through a lot in the past years and maybe he was afraid that he might pass through what he went through that year in that month, those weeks and days, he was tortured and left for hunger and thirst to finish him off.

That were the rough years of life, but then life had to move forward, justice had to be served. That day Phafoli came to the office to see TP, it had been years since they communicated, it seemed everyone had moved on with their normal lives except TP who was busy hunting criminals. Phafoli had been restored to his position in the army and everything was just moving smoothly.

"Long time no see my friend, I see you have grown", hah, hah, hah, yes TP after passing on of my wife, I had to make sure I support my kids, be there for them when ever they need me". "Yah, you are right man, so did you take another wife or you are still mourning?" "No man, I have none but there is this girl I love so much, and I guess soon I will take her in, she has been there for me you know". "Alright man, that would be great, plus children still need a mother figure near them, I am sure they have grown so much by now, last time I checked they were in high school, right?".

"Yes, yes, they have grown, the first born is doing his last year at the National University of Lesotho and the last born is in the second year in the same University". "Wow man, you have grown into a big man now". "And how about you TP, how have you been?" "Fine man, same stuff, just like old times still hunting the bad guys". "Alright man, I will invite you to my wedding soon". "Alright, I will be looking forward to it".

They parted ways. Life sometimes brings enemies together, tear apart friends, it brings the unlike charges together and things goes on, everything happens for a reason and everyone we meet. Know that one day those people might mean something into your life.

Back to work, nothing much popped up for the following two months. They had been working on trying to get closer to the minister of mining which of course they succeeded, they communicated with the army boss who was a friend of TP in service at the time to change the security personnel of the minister. And they chose their spy's within the army to be the ones who would be his body guards; they had access to everything that belonged to him, personal computers, and security cameras at home and at work, they had him by soft flesh.

In his computer, bank accounts transaction of millions of dollars in Maloti were scary, the guy had millions in different accounts, and in all the accounts he had, the money came from only one account which they couldn't find to whom exactly did it belong. "Guys, this guy is a millionaire, he can buy us and our families". TP opened his mouth widely with a surprised face when he said that, "who on earth owns about ten bank accounts, look at his older son, he is already a criminal, a kid at varsity having four bank accounts, and drive the latest cars on earth! Like father like son or maybe he is recruiting him to be the same as him".

Without any doubt the minister was dirty, they had partial evidence that could stand in court and he could be demoted from his position but that wouldn't work in their favour, they were interested in the big fish, this one was a small one, they wanted the whales or sharks, that! That would satisfy them. "If you have a friend that has a friend, that friend might be having another friend who works at the bank where the minister make his transactions, what I am trying to say is that, let us use all the resources we have, all our connections and I too will pull my former informants to find the source of money that the minister had and if we find the account, then we will find the owner and everything would be on track, otherwise the resources of this country will keep vanishing under our noses.

We are done for today, do your work at home, its Friday let's go home and rest, come Monday with clear minds and do the work". TP packed his small bag and left the office, he was so in hurry to go and see his friend at the hospital, that was each day routine, he got there in minutes and luckily Justice was already there, they set together all the visiting hours trying to make small conversations to Emm, who was just lying there, with no guarantee whether he hears what they were saying or not, with tears in their eyes they walked out as one of the nurses came to tell them that the visiting hours were over.

She needed to assess her patient; they just thanked her and departed. The following day, Phafoli's call woke TP telling him that the wedding day was near, "Sorry my friend for the short notice, I thought I still had your contacts unfortunately I lost them with my last phone, I just got them from Justice and he said he will be at the wedding too, so it's next weekend, sorry once again my friend". "Its okay man, I understand, I will be there not for you but for food and booze, you know I like food and booze right? So prepare everything".

The call ended and he got back to sleep, there wasn't much going on over the weekend, he just contacted his contacts who worked in different banks and they promised to give him feedback on Monday.

...

"The name is John Chase sir, I also ran a background check on him, he lives in South Africa Cape town with his family but he is originally from USA, he has shares in many South African gold mines, he is a gold and diamond dealer with a fleet of diamond smugglers who are in different business sectors. His people have been frequently seen in the country in the past few years which of course was the same years the mines under investigations started unaccounted losses and loosing numerous diamonds to the unknown".

"Wow, well done guys you really did a good work, I see you were busy this weekend, good work, we should start developing strategies on how to build our case to be much stronger and yes, it would be an added advantage if we catch him or his people red handed, let's proceed with our digging".

They were getting close day by day and everything was going just fine. Towards the end of the day Justice called TP saying he is outside his office waiting for him so they could go to the hospital. Loving someone is one big blessing in life, the love of friendship is one big blessing ever, winter had started , trees sheading their leaves and grass started loosing the colour, winter breeze passed through his face and Freeze his nose and ears a little as he headed to the waiting car.

It felt like that winter was going to be a strong one, clouds closed the sky and because of strong wind, clouds moved fast from one side to the other, it reminded him of that day they escaped the wrath of the army, their first mission as a great team ever created in the country. The team which sacrificed all they had to developing the country they lived up to date, many lost their lives that past years but they died in the line of duty. They will always be remembered, for they were hustlers who never gave up, some were still in prison because they were denied bail, but still they didn't give up the web because they believed in it and they knew that one day things would just be alright.

The road to the hospital was too short since TP's office was right in town and within minutes they were at the doors of the hospital. As they enter the facility, nurses and doctors ran up and down like they were dealing with a very important issue like a wounded patient so they wanted to operate him fast so as to safe his life, they were calling none stop, "Doctor room eleven hurry".

At first it didn't cross their minds what was really going on, but the number of the room sounded familiar and immediately the number eleven clicked. It was Emm's room, so they stopped making stupid assumptions and ran straight to the room, before pushing the room door, a nurse stopped them "gentlemen wait outside here, doctors are too busy in there". They obeyed, set at the chairs near the room, "one, two, three" repeated once, twice, thrice and a long sound could be heard.

Each day the sound used to be an irritating one, which kept saying tic, tic, tic, that day it just made a long tic sound and the doctor inside said "time of death is 18:19, a hot and cold something soothed their bodies, in Sesotho it is said that "monna ke nku ha alle" (the man is a sheep he doesn't cry), but sometimes you don't have a choice. Tears ran down their faces like rivers in the rainy season, they just let them because sometimes crying is the best therapy. Within minutes a doctor beckoned them to get inside the room.

"Gentlemen, we lost the fight but it's not how we anticipated things would go, we tried our best but it seems someone thought of relieving us when we thought we have worn the fight. Friday after you left he moved a finger and we were very glad of that progress, God, who could do such a thing?" TP and Justice were motionless and speechless at the same time. "What! What are you trying to imply hereDoc; we are not kids, just cut to the chase".

Before he could reply TP's question, TP's phone rang, it was a private number, "sure you admired my work, back off boy or you will regret chasing the big boys". "Who is this..." he hangs the phone. His feet went jelly like, though he didn't know who the caller was, but surely he was English by the way he talked, he returned to the room.

"I was just telling your friend that your friend here was killed, they injected him with the substance that we do not know yet because our lab technicians are still working on it, I just wonder who could do such a horrible thing!?" the doctor patted, they couldn't stop holding back their tears as they set near the bed where Emm used to sleep, "Who could do such a thing". Justice with trembling voice asked, choked by a lump in his throat as anger rages in his face.

TP wanted to  tell his friend who that might be but on the other hand he was afraid of losing his other friend, Justice was no more in the game, so if TP decides to tell him, he would blame him for his death, he would hate him forever and their friendship would just vanish. But on the other hand, telling him the truth is better than letting him discover it by himself. That would make him hate TP for good.

He was in dilemma, not knowing what to do or to say, one heart said, tell him while the other said don't. "I know who might havekilled him".  Justice raised his face surprised, "you know him!?" "Yes, that call I received, someone claimed to be responsible of the doing, and according to the way he said it I think it is related to one case we are working on at the office". "Oh man! I told you we should quit this, now you see where it has come to?". "yah I see and I am sorry, but we would never be free, this country would never be free, I think we should let go of what just happened and I will find a way to find that bustard, for I am very close to getting him".

"Let me in, let me return to work and let us do it together, I want to revenge my friend's death". "Okay justice, if you say so man, you are welcome to the team". They parted ways to their families, hot or cold, John had to be hunted down, with the help from the government or without it, but he had to be hunted.

Saturday, the wedding day was close and TP and Justice had prepared themselves

## Summary of chapter 22

This chapter, Phafoli is getting married and TP and Justice find that he is getting married to Thandi. They disappear before the wedding ends, before Phafoli and Thandi could see them. Arrange a meeting with Phafoli later telling him his wife is dirty, he refuses, he put private investigators on her but he receives no fruits. TP and Justice decide to put their own investigators on Thandi and they find he is dirty before long, tells Phafoli and he still refuses even when he sees evidence. Characters are TP, Justice, Phafoli and Thandi.

## Chapter 22

"What the hell, is this a joke, TP is this real or I am hallucinating!?" TP stood still, knowing not what to do, people were screaming with happiness, but to them, it felt like burning their lungs out, women were ululating, as soldiers hit their drums and bends, danced and do their things as like in the other wedding ceremonies where a soldier or soldiers marry.

Everything was just so fine, as everyone was merrily. But in TP and Justice were not, the pain and rage kept escalating. They didn't really know what was going on but they were invited by Phafoli who became their friend after a thousand miles they travelled together as enemies, betrayed one another but they always found a way to come to normalcy again.

"Does he know what is really going on or just like old times he jumped from being goody, goody to being Judas, or is he just betrayed like us. It looks like he doesn't know he is not seeing anything , he is so happy, smiling from ear to ear as the most beautiful lady seat besides him, oh man!, Damn, what are we going to do justice?, How do we even approach Phafoli and tell him about his wife? This girl!

The day of the wedding, Saturday, with clear sky, sun shined like a beautiful flower up the sky, birds of the air flew nicely above, while cold breeze passed swept the place, it wasn't a day a man could ware a big coat. So TP put on his dark blue suit with a dark grey shirt, put on some sun glasses, got to his car and drove off to pick Justice. Justice couldn't drive his car because the day before that one he left it at the mechanic for some repairs.

It was like they had planned on how and what to wear; they had put on dark blue suits and headed to Phafoli's home.

"This guy knows so many people, do you see the cars parked here, it's like we came to kings wedding or a well followed politician's wedding". "Yah hah, hah, hah, he is a legend TP, remember he is the right hand man of the Commander". "Yah neh!" TP and Justice talked as they seat at the table in one of tints, the tables were well decorated and everyone dressed to kill.

They had come across few people they knew, some had attend school with them at the university, while others they met through work, many were in the army and they were their former key informants, everyone was just pleased to see them. The drums and trumpets were played nicely as the bright and the groom got to their podium. Everyone ululated, stood up and cheered, the bride had a thin white lace that covered her face, she had such a beautiful body everyman would fall in love with at first glance; the groom then removed the cloth to kiss her.

Flow of hot and cold liquid like breeze rushed through their bodies that same moment, "is that Thandi!?", TP asked with disbelieve face, Justice's face was red with anger, though they haven't talked much about the day he got disappeared with Thandi at the party, TP knew that Thandi was the reason Justice got kidnapped, she was the reason that the bomb stormed their house and she was the reason Emm got into the hospital, got in coma for ten years and yes she was the reason Emm lost his life.

As they spoke, everyone was just happy, only if they would feel what was going on in their minds. Only if they could read the story of their lives on their faces, they would stop clapping their hands, stop cheering and stop smiling at the moment. The pain they underwent for the love of their county and the number of people they lost as they fought for the freedom of the country, they would just shut their mouths and start crying or maybe start running for they didn't know well the person they were ululating for.

Everything looked like a trap, a trap everyone couldn't see but TP and Justice noticed it with their two eyes that, that wasa problem, was it a trap, was it meant for them or for Phafoli? And how were they going to eliminate it. They couldn't figure out, the only way they could know was asking the person behind it.

When you want to slaughter a chicken, give it the food, one by one throw it some maize; it won't see a trap but only its food, likewise, if you want to catch a man, sent a woman. Surely Thandi thought TP and Phafoli were no longer in speaking terms for they had had long years of not talking, or maybe she knew exactly what she was doing, she knew they had started talking so that worked in her advantage. Or maybe, if one could be optimistic, she doesn't know a thing, she has left her dirty life, to be a real woman, to be a mother like other women, maybe she came clean to her husband, maybe her husband knows exactly who she was and has accepted her as she was.

But there was the only way to find out, to find straight from Thandi or Phafoli himself. The wedding was nice in general, TP and Justice made sure Thandi and Phafoli didn't see them at all and they disappeared immediately when the party started being more enjoyable. In his phone TP had missed five calls from Phafoli and Justice had his calls too. "What are we going to do man, everything is just fucked up?" Justice asked. "We call Phafoli and arrange a meeting with him tell him about his wife and see how he reacts or respond, if he knows everything, the girl came clean! Then she would be clean indeed. But if she said nothing, something big is about to happen.  Let us organize it tomorrow at the office".

The following day came, they had left Phafoli a text and he promised to be there, it was Sunday so no one was at the office, they would have a free talk. Time came and they got to the office. "Your wedding was the best man, thanks for inviting us". "You are joking TP right!? I know I invited you in a short notice but you promised to be there, that was the most important day of my life and I wanted to enjoy that day with you guys because for now I consider you my family. You should have seen my star, that woman is so beautiful, I just wish you were there".

As he said "she is the star", you could see he meant it, you can easily see when the man is in love; nothing comes in his mind except his woman, nothing he sees in his eyes but the star of his heart. That what Phafoli was like, he could easily be seen, assessed and analysed that he was deeply in love. No one would resist Thandi's beauty. That day she entered the big three's house, everyone stopped what they were doing and all eyes fell in love with her, so Phafoli like other men wouldn't resist such q beauty.

Only if he knew that behind that beauty lays pins and spears that were ready to be released and kill him, take advantage of him and get all the people he loves in trouble. Yah, only if he knew that his children were about to be in hot water because of the choice he just made, the choice of beauty over the mind, the choice of nice body over a good heart, only if he listen and listens attentively would he get out of what he was about to get into.

"What's her name before marriage man?" "She is Refiloe, why?" "She once came to our apartment and she said she was Thandi". "What! You know her?". "Listen here my friend, we were at your wedding and once we saw whom you were marrying we couldn't wait, for it would be risky for you and us, that girl have been used by Judas to perform his dirty work, so now it seems she is working with the biggest funder of Judas's master, man she is the one who let to the kidnapping of Justice. As of now we are very close to getting his big boss, we just don't know her intentions yet".

"Okay guys, hah, hah, hah, you are joking right? If you knew my wife, she is so sweet and she loves my kids and I love her, she is not all things you are saying and please, please stop". He was serious, showing the goodness of his wife, putting all the good lables on her, and decorating her with flowers. It's true that love is blind, yah, it is really blind, even if they say your wife is a monkey while in fact she is, you won't believe it because that's love, all your thinking is over clouded by love, you think of nothing else but love and all you can see is just beauty.

How do you convince someone who is in love that their lover is a danger to them and the universe? Is it by letting him taste her wrath himself, and let him suffer first?; What if they don't suffer but they lose their lives, what if he doesn't suffer at all, live a very good life, but good people, innocent people are the ones who suffer?. TP and Justice saw the problem but the problem was how to eliminate it.

"Look into our eyes Mr Phafoli". They were serious; no funny faces at all, only rage and drops of perspiration in their faces. "Do we look like we are joking? Do we always joke about things like this? I guess you have known us better than this, but it seems like you don't know us at all, but then since its hard to convince you that your wife is dirty, put a 24hour surveillance on her, watch her every move and let us find together what she is really up to".

"Okay guys, let me try that one".

...

If you want to cripple the security, any security, whether private or state security, target the information technology guys, they are core to the security system of any agency, they run day to day special operations, they run the agency itself and without them, it's just hard for the organizational body to function. In just two weeks after getting deeper into Johns investigations, TP's three IT specialists went missing, and each time one went missing he would receive a text message saying "if you want to play, then let's do it boy".

This brought frustration into the agency; everyone began wondering who would be next. Phafoli had put on private investigators on his wife and everything was just going fine, she performed wifely duties without any problems and everyone was beginning to trust her. But TP and Justice knew that, there was something very bad behind the innocence. Justice had told TP his story when he was kidnapped; he opened up after so long.

"As I was drunk in love, she asked me to disappear with her to her place and as you guys were busy we went to her house. Not long after we got in just after locking the door, about five guys came out of no where, out of other rooms, pointing guns at us. At first I thought she didn't know anything, but her smiles taught me that she organised everything. She went to the other room where she changed her clothes into all black and she immediately turned into Satan himself, she then ordered the boys 'hurry boys, I don't want to miss an important meeting, this night is too short'.

They then dragged me out to the vehicle, at the time I wished you could get out of the house and help me; I realised that everything was all organised when the other two ladies you were with came running to the vehicle. Then she said 'wait for it', and she pressed a button, and our house was on flames. I wished I could jump out of the car but I couldn't, I tried to scream my voice out but they put a cloth on my mouth and nose and I couldn't remember a thing. The next thing I woke up in that house with no windows, only a lit bulb above my head and she would come in some days and torture me, she knows her work, she is cruel, bad bitch, and my friend if you ask me if I agree with her innocent story now. I say a big no, she can't be innocent, just like that day we lay our eyes on her, she is pretending to be all innocent and we will wake up in a cage with a lion and I wonder if this time we will be lucky".

TP's mind took him to the unknown places, not knowing how they are going to get hold of that woman, on the other hand, Phafoli was convinced that his wife was Innocent, he was convinced that she was a great mother, of course that was what she really wants, that is what she was trained for, to deceive, pretend and play with the mind. She must be in the top ladder of the chain, she must be very close to her master, yah, she must be very important to her master.

"So what are we going to do man, this is much bigger and this guy really knows where and how to hit, our best IT specialists are gone, we are doing investigations but they lead us no where". TP asked, really not knowing what to do, with head in his hands, his thinking jumping from one thought to the next. "May be we should put on our own investigation and dig deeper, find her associates, you know she won't just abandon those girls she was with that day. Or just find anything that would lead us to her, let us put our own people on Phafoli's private investigators".

"Yah, you are right, maybe she has already paid off Phafoli's men".

Within no time they found that Thandi would drive out of town where she would be having secret meeting with two white guys, they don't take long time, they talk a little and she hand them some papers, which TP and the team thought might be reports. The investigators took some pictures and everything was clear that the girl was still doing her dirty work.

The thought of telling Phafoli crossed their minds, but the way the guy was in love, they wondered if it would be a good idea, he was still going to deny everything, so they couldn't waste their time telling him. With Johns case being crippled, they had to focus on what they could do and that was focusing on Thandi's moves and get her arrested or at least flip and give up her boss, if that was possible but that thinking looked like it wasn't going to see the light of the day. She was too loyal to his master and the only way to catch her was to find her red handed and that, that they could successfully reach by involving Phafoli for he was the only one close to her, who could even get to her cell phone or a hidden one because surely she wasn't using the same phone she uses for family matters.

The business one was for sure hidden. "So what are we going to do Justice, go with our initial plan, call Phafoli and show him everything that we have got?" "Yah I think we have to involve him, otherwise we are not going to get the fruits of our investigation". They proceeded with the later plan, arranged a meeting with Phafoli and got down with business.

"Man, everything you need to be convinced that your wife is dirty is here, photos, everything from our investigations unit and we need to act fast, otherwise she will achieve her goal very soon and we won`t be able to catch forever". Phafoli at the time had opened his eyes widely, he could be seen he was fuming with anger, which was understandable; everyman could react the same way after discovering that they have been played by the person they loved or love dearly.

He even trembled a little, by the look of his trousers which vibrated like Nokia 3310, or like he was standing next to the Air con, he then raised his hand pointing his finger at TP and Justice, with anger written in his eyes, "So you guys have been doing your own investigations on my wife behind my back, I told you I could handle her, you just thought I was a mad man you could go behind his back".

TP and Justice were confused, not knowing what to say or do. They say love is blind but sometimes it`s stupid, how could you defend someone even when every evidence has been provided, how? Or maybe she gave him 'Phehla' (traditional herb given by women to husband's so that they can submit to them). This one was really out of control, at the time Phafoli had left them standing in the office, threw papers that were in his hands furiously on the table and headed to the door, slammed it and got to his car and accelerated up the street.

By the sound of the car tires at the road, everyone could feel that the guy was angry, but what for? Sometimes truth hurts, accepting reality is one big thing many people don't want to face and most of the time they spend their whole lives living fake lives, living other people's lives without taking control of the situations around them. And that was what Phafoli was doing, running away from truth. But the fact about truth is that, it always comes back to haunt you, that is why many people before they die, they confess first about the facts of their lives.

This is why we are advised to go and confess our sins in churches before priest. It is the only reason we are doing that, let go our sins; lies and start a new life, the truthful life. TP and Justice were disappointed but they couldn't stop doing their work, many people had lost their lives giving their all to this country, hustled so much to making it what it is today, so they couldn't just give up over that miner set back, they had to come back and that didn't take long time than they anticipated because...

## Summary of chapter 23

In this chapter, Phafoli agrees to dig deep into his wife's things; they put a 24hrs team that guards her so that she could not be of danger to him and the kids. He finds the phone she uses to communicate with her employers; she catches him, and shoots him on the spot. The teams rush to the house, Thandi confesses to everything, she says she killed Emm and then she shoots herself in the head. The following day John, minister of mining and other officials get arrested but TP is still troubled by Thandi's final words. Characters are TP, Phafoli, Thandi, Justice, and the officer.

## Chapter 23

At first they thought their ears were deceiving them, but looking closely at the house, gun shots were coming straight from the house, lights were off so it could be seen very well as the gun fires. All the teams rushed to the house very fast. In fighting or in a battle, most people who get injured or die are the innocent, are the good people, and the bad ones always find a way to make it alive or even if they die, they sometimes die honourable deaths because they are perceived to be heroes while in reality are the ones who let to the deaths of the innocent.

A day after TP, Justice and Phafoli had a meeting, unexpected call from Phafoli got to TP's phone, "man I am very sorry by the way I acted at the office that day, I just couldn't cope with the truth, the thought of losing that woman gave me headache, but on the other hand, I see she is a danger to me and my children. I know what I did to you guys might have pieced you off, but if there is anything I can do to set things right, to help you with the investigations, please let me know".

There is nothing that humbles a soul than apologising after realizing that you have wronged someone and Phafoli's apology was right on time, when boys were busy developing strategies on what they could do so as to catch their fish, they had agreed with the army boss and police commissioner to put a 24hrs surveillance at Phafoli's home so that the wife couldn't be of any danger to him and the kids.

"Alright man, first things first, find a phone she uses to contact with her employer, don't make her suspicious, do not confront her on anything related to her movements, and act as normal as you can". "Okay TP, I will try my best". That day in the evening he was supposed to start looking for the phone, so teams were waiting outside; about 2hrs went by without a call from Phafoli telling whether he found anything or not, after few hours he called...

"I got the phone and everything is... 'What are you doing Phafoli?' 'I am talking to a friend; I couldn't call him in the bed room avoiding waking you'. Hell had broken out to the underground, the voice from the background was from Phafoli's wife, and it seemed he was caught; he didn't even get a time to switch his phone off. "No I mean what are you doing with my phone on the other hand? You have gone too far this time, I tried to be the best woman I could be for you but all you do is to search my things while I sleep".

"Okay, tell me then, what are you doing with the second phone and why are you hiding it?" that is Phafoli trying to defend himself. "Sure you have opened it Phafoli and checked everything in it, what does it look like, I am sure you have made your own conclusions, but for your information, everything you saw in that phone is true, I am not what you thought I was, I am not the woman you thought I was, but as time went on, I fell in love with you".

"Just shut the fuck up, all this time you have been pretending to love me and my kids and you think I am going to fall with the lies you are telling me now!". "Well, in that case, you leave me no choice Phafoli but to do what I am best at". "what are you doing, we can talk about this, let's go to the police together and come clean, give up whoever is using you and everything will be alright, please don't do what you will regret later".

Via the phone TP and the teams could hear Phafoli was in trouble, but they couldn't figure well what was going on, so they stood by a little longer thinking maybe she would submit to Phafoli's trap. "you know, you used to be the best agent Phafoli, I didn't have to come down to the field to get dust on my boots, you were the best at what you did, I know you didn't even know who really hired you, for you thought it was that fat politician, you were really good and I admired you for that, then you found that rubbish called TP and you broke my heart, but what broke my heart even more is that, you are trying to help them with their investigations so as to bring my boss down; yah, you thought I didn't know, I know everything about you, your every move and the meetings you have been having with them...

So I found myself hating you more and more, day by day, such that sometimes I just wanted to kill you in your sleep, but that wouldn't please me. I wanted to look you in the eyes and see how you would react as death knocks in your heart". "We can solve this and figure the way out of it babe..." before he could finish, gun shots were heard multiple times and all the teams rushed to the house, the whole place was completely surrounded and there was no way she could escape.

They forcefully kicked down the door, got in the house and found Phafoli on the floor in the pool of his blood, lying still on the floor; they rushed to the bedroom where they found Thandi seating on the bed with the gun in her hands, not pointing to anyone but to herself. "Please just stop, it's over, your life first, just give us your boss and everything will be fine, who knows, you might walk free". that`s One officer trying his luck. "Just stop, I am tired of everything, I told Phafoli I was beginning to fall in love with him and I was serious, I wanted to set things right in my life and I was performing my last mission and getting out of all this mess...

But now with Phafoli dead, I have no reason to live at all, even if I chose to stay for his children, how am I going to face them, how are they going to face me after all I did? I wish he could wake up so that I could tell him how sorry I am, but then it's the path we all share, it's an in evitable thing we all have to go through, and guys I lived my life the way I wanted, I wasn't forced to do all the things I did, I chose them myself and I liked it. I saw men and women fall by my hand and I just felt nothing...

You might think you are closer to catching my boss, but guys, this is way bigger than yourselves, this is not a one man mission, everything I tell you now is the truth and truth only. This is way bigger than you think and like it or not, they are going to capture this country and you wont be able to do anything about it. And finally, I am very sorry for your friend, it's me who killed him in the hospital".

No one moved, everyone listened attentively, surprised at what Thandi was saying, and everyone reflecting at his own life wondering where would their lives lead them and how would they die..Boom! Their thoughts were interrupted by a gun shot, and

Thandi in seconds was lying on bed with stream of blood coming down her head. We don't choose how we die and when we would die but it is amazing that other people get to choose their own way of dying, live the way they want and die the way they want.

Thandi lived her life by her own terms and rules, even in the end she chose her own way of dying. She was still holding a phone in her hand and checking the text messages, she was to have a meeting with John in one hotel in Maseru, and everything was already arranged, the time and where they would find one another. It's surprising that she didn't even call or text John to tell him that he should cancel the meeting and run, maybe she had truly changed.

The following day John was arrested at the spot where they were supposed to meet with Thandi, and he was charged along with the minister of mining and some other officials. But in TP's mind, Thandi's words kept replaying, "this is way bigger than yourselves, this is not a one man's mission, like it or not, they will capture this country and you will do nothing about it".

These words gave him a headache, he couldn't think of anything but her last words. The way to freedom seemed to be a very long one, it requires a great hustler, such that sometimes he doubted himself but then thought to himself, "I will hustle for their freedom, I will hustle and never stop, even if I fall I will fall hustling for them, for the hustler's story Never die, even the coming generations will know that I fought for this land and I didn't hustle for nothing.

**END**

www.ingramcontent.com/pod-product-compliance
Lightning Source LLC
Chambersburg PA
CBHW061237140726

47998CB00006B/2012